Thomas Jefferson Jenkins

Side Switches of the Short Line

Thomas Jefferson Jenkins

Side Switches of the Short Line

ISBN/EAN: 9783337393946

Printed in Europe, USA, Canada, Australia, Japan

Cover: Foto ©Andreas Hilbeck / pixelio.de

More available books at **www.hansebooks.com**

SIDE SWITCHES

OF THE

SHORT L E

JOINTLY BY

REV. J. W. BOOK

AND

REV. THOS. JEFFERSON JENKINS.

NINTH EDITION.

ST. LOUIS, MO. 1905.
PUBLISHED BY B. HERDER,
17 SOUTH BROADWAY.

PREFACE NOTES.

The authors of this first sequel to the SHORT LINE TO THE ROMAN CATHOLIC CHURCH have had such material proofs of the favor of clergy and laity in the prompt sale of the original book of the SHORT LINE SERIES, that they feel it unnecessary to do more than express their gratitude for such wide-spread appreciation.

It has been our purpose to avoid harsh controversy, and to conduct our discussions with our separated brethren in the kindest, if firmest, manner.

We try to answer strong statements of objections by a full and clear exposition of the Church's doctrine and practices, in the language best understood and popular among non-Catholics.

Naught is set down in malice—God forbid! Nor do we indulge, as we freely challenge the unprejudiced reader to judge from the following pages, in any rancorous or sarcastic expressions.

Finally, we bring to bear on the various disputed questions, especially in the historical line, almost exclusively non-Catholic authorities. And in connection with the Church's Dogmas, Sacraments and Sacred Rites we use only authorized manuals and rituals.

Advancing in the sale of the SHORT LINE to the NINTH EDITION, twenty-fifth thousand, we hope this SIDE-SWITCHES and succeeding Booklets on select questions of interest may be as largely distributed.

THE JOINT AUTHORS.

CONTENTS.

(4)

SIDE-SWITCHES OF THE SHORT LINE.

BOOKLET FIRST—BRANCH ROADS.

I. THE LUTHERAN FIRST.

CHARACTERS REPRESENTED.

Lutheran—Pastor.	*Baptist—Exhorter.*
Episcopalian—Archdeacon.	*Methodist—Bro. Wesley.*
Presbyterian—Mr. Knox.	*Roman Catholic—Father.*

Pastor: "Rev. Father, addressing you familiarly, we spent a very pleasant evening yesterday in perusing the SHORT LINE TO THE ROMAN CATHOLIC CHURCH."

Father: "Indeed! For an author this is quite refreshing. As a rule, his feelings are not often spared, though they are as sensitive as those of people following other avocations."

Pastor: "It is true, your little work is an eye-opener to us; but, Father, this does not mean that we consider it faultless. With your permission, I ask for myself and the Rev. spokesmen of the other denominations perfect freedom of speech in this discussion."

Father: "Certainly, Rev. Pastor and gentlemen, I shall treat you with the respect due your convictions, and I expect the same gentlemanly courtesy from you. Our regard for one another need not interfere with plain talk and bold defense of each one's church. I think our general motto may be: 'Spare feelings, but give no quarter to false doctrines.'"

Exhorter: "Yes, sir, for my part, I do not wish to be hampered in expresssing my opinion."

Father: "By the way, do you gentlemen agree among yourselves; in other words, do you believe alike in every particular?"

Bro. Wesley: "Not at all, sir; we are Protestants, and this means, 'think for yourselves.'"

Father: "Very encouraging, indeed."

Pastor: "How so, Father?"

Father: "*United we stand, divided we fall.* I am not afraid of you singly. But, to fight you united might be a harder task."

Archdeacon: "Rev. Father, as to a moderator?"

Father: "I do not think we need an umpire other than the public of this broad, free land. However, as to the origin of each denomination, let ordinary history, admitted on all hands as substantially true, be received as authority without appeal."

Archdeacon: "There can surely be no objection to so plain an understanding. I believe, though, the gentlemen will demand that their several books of Confessions and Articles of Faith shall be admitted as witnesses of what each church holds as to its origin."

Father: "By all means, Archdeacon, and we Catholics are willing to be judged by the definitions and decrees of the Church as set forth by the Pope, its Head, and by General Councils; but, remember, Rev. Sirs, that this question is mainly, if not merely, an historical one; and we shall confine the debate to the question, 'Which Church can prove by the test of history that it was founded by Christ and comes down unchanged from the Apostles?' "

Archdeacon: "Gentlemen, are we all agreed as to the subject, and the methods mentioned?" (Carried unanimously.)

Archdeacon: "l notice, then, Father, you have challenged us to prove our title to be called *Branches* of the True Church. We Episcopalians form one of these Branches. My reasons are the following:"—

Father: "Would it not be proper to leave the floor to our Lutheran friend?"

Pastor: "Dr. Martin Luther was the *first* to revolt against the abuses of the Church and the aggressions of the Pope of Rome. You, Rev. Archdeacon, will concede that your Anglican Branch was grafted on the main stem by Henry VIII, or rather by Queen Elizabeth, when *we* had already been in the field a score of years. Therefore, by virtue of priority, the Father must be right in giving me the floor."

Archdeacon: "I believe myself it will be better to allow the Pastor to proceed."

Pastor: "Thank you all kindly; especially you, Rev. Father, for the implied admission that we were the *first* in the field."

Father: "I am willing to acknowledge the Lutheran priority. You know, I know, and the world knows, that Henry VIII received at the hands of the then reigning Pope the title of *Defender of the Faith*, precisely as the reward for his tilt against Dr. Martin Luther. To this day, the queen of England carries this title; but, excuse me, Archdeacon, unjustly, as we shall see later on. Remember, however, Rev.

Pastor, *we* were on the grounds when *you* came. Therefore, I shall put you on the defensive. It will devolve upon you to show that we were wrong. Tell us about the origin of your Church. I believe you have already intimated that Dr. Martin Luther laid the first Side-switch off the Main Line, the Roman Catholic Church. By the way, when was Luther born?"

Pastor: "In 1483, at Eisleben, Saxony."

Father: "Rather late in the day. Of course you do not claim that Martin Luther founded your Church in the days of his boyhood. Therefore, it must have been fully 1500 years after the coming of Christ that your Church was established. We Catholics do not believe in a Church founded by a mere man—we prefer the one established by the Redeemer of the World, now more than 1800 years ago."

Archdeacon: "You are right, Father. You Catholics and we Episcopalians agree on this question. A Church established by a mere man is no Church at all."

Pastor: "Beg your pardon, Archdeacon. Both you and the Father misunderstand us. Strictly speaking, Luther was not the founder of a new Church, but the reformer of one that had fallen into grossest errors. The words *founder* and *reformer* must not be confounded. Most probably, no doubt, you have read *Why I Am What I Am*, published by J. S. Ogilvie, in 1891, New York City. In it fourteen clergymen give reasons for the faith that is in them. The Rev. G. F. Krodel, D.D., of the Holy Trinity, is the author of the article: *Why I Am a Lutheran.* Let him speak for himself:

While there were reformers before the Reformation, and Ulrich Zwingli was at work in Switzerland
at the very. time when Luther at Wittenberg was
earnestly contending *for the faith which was once delivered
unto the saints*, it cannot be questioned that Luther,
after all, was the greatest and most commanding
figure in the Reformation of the sixteenth century,
and that its first and most decisive battles were fought
on German ground and under his leadership. His
name became the war-cry of the friends of reform
and the stigma which its foes attached to all his followers.

Says Buddens: Whilst Luther amended the grav-
est errors and vices of the Church of Rome and
restored the church to a happier condition, he did
not frame a new church.

The doctrine of the Lutherans, • says Welch, "is
no new doctrine; it is the same which has been stead-
fastly preserved in the church from of old, and from
the times of the apostles, for we teach nothing in our
churches, except what the pure, ancient apostolic
Christian church teaches."

Father: "Please tell me what you understand by
Reformation; does it consist in reforming the morals
of the people, or in changing the articles of faith?"

Pastor: "In both. You must admit that in the
time of the Reformation the morals of the people
were very loose, and, as to the teachings of the
Church, you need not be told that the condition was
no better."

Father: As to the morals of the people at the time
of the Reformation, the following must be taken into
consideration:

1.   *Evil always excites more attention and makes more
noise in the world than good.* For this reason, real or
imaginary abuses are highly colored by the opposing
party

2. To quote Archbishop Spalding: 'Abuses and scandals generally originated in the world and its princes, not in the Church and its chief pastors; most of them being due to the fact that bad men were thrust into the high places of the Church by the wordly-minded and avaricious princes in spite of the Popes, whose settled policy it was to protest with all their might against a line of conduct so very ruinous to the best interests of religion.'

Be this as it may, the Catholic Church has never objected and never will object to a reformation in favor of morality. She is the custodian of morals. Every sermon she preaches, every lesson taught, every book she prints, every school and church she erects has for its object the eradication of vice and the promotion of morals.

As to the reformation concerning articles of faith, we shall speak later. Tell me what do you think about the propriety of Martin Luther setting himself up as a reformer of morals? Being told by you when he was born, you may tell us what he was and how he stood in society."

Pastor: "Gladly shall I do so. He was not only a Catholic, but a priest, and to cap it all, an Augustinian monk. Therefore, he must have been well aware of the *real condition* of the Church; therefore, he set on foot the grandest and most glorious reformation the world has ever seen or ever will see."

Father: "Stop, my friend, you are getting too eloquent. Let us keep cool, bring the matter in question before the tribunal of reason, and by all means not overlook historical facts, related by non-Catholic writers. We prefer quoting them rather than Catholics, and, surely, you cannot object to them. At the start Luther did not intend that the Reformation should be so sweeping as it proved to be in the end. You remember that on the 1st of November, 1517, he published ninety-five theses against Tetzel, the Dominican. In the 38th, 67th and 71st of these he upheld the Pope's authority and adhered to the Catholic doctrine on indulgences. By and by he fell deeper, though his conscience troubled him not a little—he admits it himself: 'How often has my conscience disturbed me? How often have I said to myself: dost thou imagine thyself wiser than the rest of mankind? Darest thou imagine that all of mankind have been in error for so long a series of years?' (*Opp. Lutheri* Germ. Edit. Geneva, vol. II, fol. 9.) Again: 'I am not so bold as to assert that I have been guided in this affair by God; upon this point I would not wish to undergo the judgment of God.' (Ibid, vol. I, p. 364.) Had Luther confined himself to the reformation of some national abuses, no objections would have been raised to him from a Catholic standpoint. On the contrary, he would have been lauded to the skies. But, he began to remove the landmarks of faith, set up by Christ Himself and His Apostles. Apart from this, however, do you believe Martin Luther possessed the necessary qualities to reform even the morals of the people?"

Pastor: "I do, indeed. Like the prophets of old, he must have enjoyed the special protection of Divine Providence."

Exhorter: "One thing I do know, Luther knew nothing about baptism. On this question we Baptists alone are right. *We do not believe in baptizing behind the stove.*"

Bro. Wesley: "I have something to say also. However, just now let the Father and the Pastor fight it out. The more opinions the more confusion."

Father: "I agree with you, Bro. Wesley. Let us, therefore, Rev. Pastor, come to the point in question. For my part, I do not believe God, who is essentially holy, could have chosen a man like Luther to reform His own work."

Pastor: "I can not see how a well-meaning man could object to Martin Luther, who unchained the Bible and gave us once more the pure word of God—who restored the Church to its primitive purity."

Father: "Luther admits in his treatise, *De Missa Privata*, that he had a *conference with the devil*. Either this is true, or it is not true; if it is, he moved in bad society; if it is not, he handled the truth roughly. In either case he could not have been chosen by the God of truth and sanctity to reform the Church, divinely instituted.

What shall I say of Luther's *Table Talk*, of which the first edition appeared at Eisleben in 1566? I have a copy printed in 1700, right there in my library. Should you ever wish to make use of it, you may do so. I must confess it disgusts me to read it. In the Eisleben edition, p. 213, we read the following: 'May the name of the Pope be d—d; may his reign be abolished; may his will be restrained! If I thought that God did not hear my prayer I would address the devil.' Again: 'I owe more to my dear Catharine and to Philip than to God Himself.' (Ibid, p. 124.) Finally: 'God has made many mistakes. I would have given him good advice had I assisted at the creation. I would have made the sun shine incessantly;

the day would have been without end.' (Ibid Edit.
Frank., part II., fol. 20.) Who would look upon
Luther as an ambassador of God when he utters these
blasphemies.''

Pastor: ''To deny these historical facts would be
rashness on my part. However, you must take the
spirit of the times into consideration. Remember,
Luther was a child of his day. The corruption of the
age was so general that it was impossible to keep
one's self uncontaminated. Think of the bad Popes
in the Roman Church.''

Father: ''In the first place, these Popes belonged
to you as well as to us. You admitted a while ago
that Luther was a priest, and before the Reformation
there were no Lutherans.

In the second place, you will never hear us call
bad Popes good Popes. But you praise Luther *sine
fine*—to the bitter end. Therefore, I have a right to
show by his own statements that you are misled. *By
their fruits you shall know them.*

Furthermore, his immoral conduct is in perfect
accord with his utterances, which, in themselves,
might be more or less excused, since we know he was
in the habit of imbibing too freely. I need not call
your attention to his song: *Wein, Weib und Gesang.*
On the other hand, I can not refrain from calling to
your mind his well-known marriage with Catharine
Bora, who had vowed virginity as well as himself. In
short, a man who blasphemes; who, having the beer
mug always in his hand, uses foul language, breaks
the vows made by himself; who enters the sacred cell
consecrated by the vows of virginity and robs its in-
mate of her most precious jewel—a man who does all

this and more, can not be a reformer of the Church
of God. Martin Luther is guilty of all this. Therefore, he is not a reformer; therefore, he should be
stigmatized as an impostor and destroyer of immortal
souls; therefore, all those who uphold him participate
in his infamous and nefarious work that depopulates
heaven and replenishes hell."

Pastor: "Now, Father, if I have been too *eloquent,*
you are so none the less. In this world there is a
limit to everything. Sometimes the very best people
will overstep the bounds. This is what Luther did
when he took the vows to which you refer. However,
he had the manliness to retrace his steps as soon as
the scales fell from his eyes."

Father: "The vow that Luther made was a *free
and solemn promise, made to God, to do something that
he was not otherwise obliged to do.* Now, we maintain
that such a promise is binding on the conscience, and
we prove this from the Scriptures, which Luther
claims to have placed within the reach of the people.
'When thou hast made a vow to the Lord thy God,
thou shalt not delay to pay it; because the Lord thy
God will require it. And if thou delay, it shall be
imputed to thee for a sin.' (Deuteronomy c. 23,
v. 21). 'He that giveth his virgin in marriage, doeth
well; and he that giveth her not, doeth better.'
(I. Cor. 7: 33). St. Paul was not married. He gives
every man his own choice; but he wishes 'that all
men were even as himself.' St. John, the beloved
disciple of Christ, followed the example of his Divine
Master. Not to marry, therefore, is better than the
contrary; therefore, a free solemn promise made to
this effect is a vow which must be held sacred; there-

fore, Dr. M. Luther sinned in taking Catharine Bora for a wife; therefore he was not a *reformer*, but a *deformer* of morals."

Pastor: "Since I am not prepared to argue the question just now, let it pass under the plea of *difference of opinion.*"

Father: "After making one more remark, I am willing to do so, for it surely is a misfortune that history had to record this chapter in his life. What I wish to add is this: Luther himself, in his sober moments, did not approve of his own marriage. M. Audin, quoting authentic documents, says: 'After the labors of the day, he would walk with Catharine. * * * One evening the stars sparkled with unwonted brightness, and the heavens appeared to be on fire. *Behold, what splendor those luminous points emit,* said Catharine to Luther. Luther raised his eyes: *What glorious light!* * * * *it shines not for us. Why not?* replied Bora, *have we lost our title to the Kingdom of Heaven?* Luther sighed: *Perhaps so* * * * *because we have abandoned our state. We ought to return to it then,* said Catharine. *It is too late* * * * *the cart is too deep in the mud,* added the Doctor.' But Luther was not only licentious himself. He granted the same unrestrained liberties to others; for instance, to Philip, Landgrave of Hesse."

Pastor: "According to St. Paul, a Christian" *conversation is in heaven;* but you, Father, are always harping on vices. How is it that you can see nothing good in other people, especially if they do not belong to the Roman Catholic Church?

Father: "You came here with the avowed intention of convincing me that Luther was the instrument used by Almighty God to purify His church. Now, before you leave me, I am determined to convince you to the contrary. 'Luther and the seven other theologians informed the Prince (Landgrave of Hesse), that they could not sanction the universal introduction of polygamy.' 'Your Highness will yourself see clearly enough, what difference there is between making a universal law and making use of a dispensation in a certain case for grave reasons, and by virtue of a divine concession. But no dispensation, granted in opposition to God, can be valid.' (De Wette, 237-236.)

'Finally, if your Highness has altogether made up your mind to marry another wife, we declare under oath, that it ought to be done secretly * * * This modest way of living would please more than adultery * * * Nor are the sayings of others to be cared for if our conscience is in order. Thus and thus far only do we approve of it.' (Ibidem, 241.)

To this says Koestlin, Luther's greatest champion: 'It is the greatest blot in the history of the Reformation and in the life of Luther.'

Pastor, what do you think of this episode? How do these words sound in the mouth of a Reformer? Luther stands very low in the estimation of his co-reformers.''

Exhorter: "This is something new to me. I dare say many Protestants have never heard anything about this double marriage of the Landgrave. Excuse me for interrupting the conversation. This discussion is getting to be quite monotonous. I think we, the representatives of other denominations, should have the privilege of throwing in a word or two occasionally.

It is hard to keep silence when you have something good to say."

Archdeacon: "I am of the same opinion. Therefore let me break the monotony. You are right, Rev. Father, when you make the statement that Luther's co-reformers objected to many of his ways and means. For example, Henry VIII. writes: 'I wonder no more, O Luther, that thou art not in good earnest ashamed, and that thou darest to lift up thine eyes either before God or men * * * Thou a brother of the order of St. Augustine, hast been the first to abuse a consecrated nun.' " (In Horim. p. 299.)

Pastor: "Archdeacon! I am surprised that yo call on Henry in this delicate matter. His matrimonial career was anything but edifying."

Father: "Never mind, Rev. Pastor, when the Archdeacon has the floor, we shall gently remin' him of the mistake he has made."

Knox: "Calvin, cited by Conrad Schlussemberg says: *In very truth, Luther is extremely corrupt.*"

Bro. Wesley: "Since you all have had your turn, let me *now* claim mine. Zwingli says of Luther: 'To see him in the midst of his followers, you would believe him possessed by a phalanx of devils.' " (T. II. Respons. ad Confess. Lutheri fol. 381.)

Pastor: "Look here! Did we not come to this house with the intention of convincing the Father that the SHORT LINE is misleading, that it may lead weak-minded people into the Church of Rome, but never into the Church of God? Therefore we must avoid the very appearance of war in our own camp. In this way we shall never convince the world of the glorious truths of the Gospel, so long withheld from the *dear* people."

Exhorter: "Of course, I firmly believe the people of God were kept for many centuries in darkness; but when we look at the life of Luther in the light of history, it would be folly to try to hoodwink the Father. You see it frequently happens that our opponents study our history better than we do ourselves. To tell the truth, I should hate to be either a Catholic or a Lutheran; for I believe in my heart both are wrong."

Father: "Since the opinion seems to be prevalent, that Luther·personally does not deserve the title of a gentleman, much less of a reformer, and, consequently, not likely to be employed in this capacity by a God of sanctity, let us consider the Reformation from another aspect. A man might possibly lead a bad life and yet teach sound doctrines. We ourselves, believe this of a few Popes. You may proceed, Rev. Pastor."

Pastor: "I think so too. If Luther was an immoral man, of which I am not yet by any means convinced, he may have pointed out the doctrine of salvation. This I shall try to prove now, and rest assured, that my confreres will raise no objections to the doctrines promulgated by the Father of the Reformation. Let us begin with the infamous doctrine of *indulgences*, which Leo X. granted in the beginning of the sixteenth century, and which was the prime cause of the ever-glorious reformation. No man that has any self-respect can approve of this damnable traffic."

Father. "It seems to me, my friend, you confound two things; the doctrine and the sale of indulgences.

As far as the doctrine of *indulgences* is concerned, see the SHORT LINE to the ROMAN CATHOLIC CHURCH, advertised in this book. Let me add, however, that Luther himself, as I said before, did not attack the dogma itself. (Thesis 71.) In other words, he believed in indulgences, which are neither a remission of sin nor a license to commit sin, as many non-Catholics will tell you.

On the other hand, the traffic in *indulgences* would be *simony*, (see eighth chap. of the Acts of Apostles.) which has been condemned by the Church most severely before and after Luther's time. To bring proof for this would be to insult the student of ecclesiastical history. Waiving Tetzel's conduct as to the administration of the promulgated indulgence. Church authorities never have approved and never will approve of their sale. It is a crime most sinful.

To-day you Lutherans do not believe in *indulgences*; consequently, you are bound to admit, either that God did not send the Doctor to reform His Church or that He made known the truth piece-meal, in other words, mixed up truth with falsehood. The one is as much opposed to an essential attribute of God as the other—I mean sanctity?"

Exhorter: "Look here, Pastor, can't you speak of something else? I have heard and read so much about *indulgences* that I can not bear to hear them mentioned."

Archdeacon: "I am also of this opinion, Rev. Pastor. Drop the question—it is old and stale.

speak to the Father about Bible reading. He knows and we know it is a blessing conferred upon us by the Reformation."

Pastor: "Father, no man will have the hardihood to deny that. prior to Luther, the Bible containing God's holy word was an *unknown* book."

Archdeacon: "Of course, I too believe Rome has never treated the Bible with due respect, but I must confess you are handling the truth a little recklessly when you claim it to have been an *unknown* book. Remember, this statement provoked a smile from one of our greatest and most renowned English Protestant writers, Dr. Maitland. Says he: 'To say nothing of parts of the Bible, or of books whose place is uncertain, we know of at *least twenty* different editions of the whole Latin Bible, printed in *Germany only*, before Luther was born. These had issued from Augsburg, Strasburg, Cologne, Ulm, Mentz, Basle, Nuremberg and were dispersed through Germany. I repeat, before Luther was born . . . . . And yet   . . . . we find a young man who had received a *liberal education*, who *had made great proficiency in his studies at Magdeburg, Eisenach and Erfurth*, and who, nevertheless, did not know what a Bible was, simply because *the Bible was unknown in those days*!' (The Dark Ages, etc., p. 469, notes.) Excuse me, I am so great an admirer of Dr. Maitland that I can not refrain from quoting this passage."

Pastor: "No doubt, Rev. Father, you understand me, but it seems the Archdeacon does not. Of course, I am well aware of the fact that, all things being taken into consideration, Latin Bibles were rather plentiful; but remember, only priests were masters or this language; consequently the people, the poor people, were prevented from drawing spiritual consolation from this refreshing source."

Father: "Pastor, you are again mistaken. At the time of the Reformation it was quite common to meet Latin scholars; it was the mother tongue of our own Columbus. Furthermore, publishers will not print books to have them shelved. This is a well-known fact. Now Seckendorf, in his *Commentaries on Lutheranism*, admits that three distinct German editions of the Bible appeared in 1480, 1483 and 1490 at Wittenberg. Remember, this took place shortly before and shortly after Luther was born. Menzel is so honest as to say in his *History of Germany*, vol. II, p. 223: 'Before the time of Luther the Bible had already been translated and printed in both High and Low Dutch.' France and Italy also had their translations."

Archdeacon: "The English people are well aware of the fact that the Ven. Bede left them a translation in the eighth and John De Trevisa in the fourteenth century."

Father: "The Very Rev. Father Seepe, of Madison, Ind., has a German Bible printed at Nuremberg in the spring of 1483, before Luther was born.

I cannot go into detail for want of time and space. Read *Janssen's Geschichte des Deutschen Volkes* or the *History of the Reformation* by Spalding, and you will be surprised to see into how many languages the Bible had been translated, not to speak of the many editions, before and during the time of Dr. Martin Luther. Therefore, you Lutherans have been badly imposed upon. Luther's *literary* work on the German

Bible can be commended, however; he corrupted many a sacred text.''

Pastor: ''Now, Father, you surely do not mean what you say!''

Father: ''I do, indeed. Luther, I repeat it, corrupted the sacred Word of God, and his co-reformers do not deny it. Says Bucer: 'His falls in translating and explaining the Scriptures were manifest and not a few.' (Dial. contra Melancthon.) Zwingli is not afraid to say that Luther's Bible is a corruption of the Word of God. Hallam, whose Protestantism will not be questioned by any one, says: 'The translation of the Old and New Testament by Luther is more re-- nowned for the purity of the German idiom than for its adherence to the original text.'

This is easily demonstrated. Not to mention the fact that he looks upon the Epistle of St. James as an *Epistle of Straw*, he inserts the word *alone* in the 28th verse of the III. Chap. of St. Paul to the Romans: 'So we now hold it, that man is justified, without doing the works of the law, *alone* through faith.' (Original Wittenberg edition of 1522.) Luther admits having done this in a letter to Wenceslaus Link: 'If your Papist makes much unnecessary fuss about the word (*alone*), say straight out to him, Doctor Martin Luther will have it so, and says, Papists and donkeys are one and the same thing. Sic volo, sic jubeo, stat pro ratione voluntas (thus I will have it, thus I order it, my will is reason enough). For we will not be the scholars or the disciples of the Papists, but their masters and judges. We must once in a way act a little haughtily and noisily with these

jackasses.' *(Send-brieff von * * * Fuerbitle
Der Heiligen*, Wittenberg, 1530).''

Pastor: ''You say in your SHORT LINE TO THE
ROMAN CATHOLIC CHURCH, that the Bible was not the
Rule of Faith in the time of Christ and the Apostles.
For this statement you gave a good reason. You also
said, that for the want of Bibles, it could not be the
rule during the first 1500 years of the Christian era.
This also seems very plausible. But after the art of
printing was invented, I know of no other *Rule of
Faith* better than the Bible, and for this Rule we
must give the Father of the Reformation credit, even
if he has made some blunders.''

Father: ''Thank you for the adn.ission that from
your standpoint the Christians were groping in the
dark for 1500 years—in other words had no *reliable
teacher.*''

Archdeacon: ''Were I the Pastor I should never
admit it; but, go on, Father.''

Father: ''The admission is made and the word of
a representative man ought to be good. As to the
Bible being the *Rule of Faith*, let us put it to a practical test. You will remember, during the Reformation there was quite a squabble in regard to the Lord's
supper. What is the Lord's supper, or Holy
Eucharist, as we call it in our catechism?''

Pastor: ''Of course, as to the Sacrament there
was, at one time, quite a difference of opinion.
Luther believed in what the Latins called *impanatio*
—that is, he taught explicity that the body of our
Lord Jesus Christ is truly and substantially present in
the bread, but that the latter remains unchanged—
remains bread.

Bro. Wesley: "Evidently this was Martin Luther's doctrine on the question. For in 1544 he published a little work of 44 pages, in which he makes his profession in regard to the Lord's supper. Says he, against Zwingli and the other Sacramentarians: 'I would have known well * * * how to give them their proper name, as being not only devourers of bread and swallowers of wine, but devourers of souls and murderers of souls, and as having a satanical, a thoroughly satanical, a supersatanical, blasphemous heart and a lying mouth.' Again: 'I should have to condemn myself with them into the depths of Hell, were I to hold with them, or to have communion with them, or were I to be silent if I find out or hear that they boasted of being in communion with me. The devil and his mother may do that, or be silent in such a case (*dazu*), but not I.' Indeed, this is forcible language, but it is *a la* Luther. We know he was not afraid to express his convictions."

Pastor: "Unfortunately, the first Reformers did not always agree among themselves. Zwingli denies the real presence of Christ. According to his explanation our Savior's words mean, *This signifies my body.*"

Knox: "And, according to my views, both were wrong. Calvin's views are mine. He teaches that in the Lord's supper we are united to Christ by faith only. Therefore, we read in the *Confession of Faith* of the Presbyterians: 'They that worthily communicate in the Sacrament of the Lord's supper do therein feed upon the body and blood of Christ, not after a corporal or carnal, but in a spiritual manner; yet truly and really, while by faith they receive and apply unto themselves Christ crucified and all the benefits of his death.' "

Father: "Archdeacon, what have you to say about this? I notice in the Confession of Faith of the Presbyterians that the Lord's supper is called a sacrament. Do you also consider it so?"

Archdeacon: "With us everything is well defined. Our Thirty-nine Articles have been assailed on every side. But to this day they are as solid, as immovable as ever. They have stood and they will stand. Let me call the attention of you gentlemen to the twenty-eighth article: 'The supper of the Lord is not only a sign of the love that Christians ought to have among themselves one to another, but rather is a Sacrament of our Redemption by Christ's death.' "

Knox: "Excuse me for the interruption. You may consider this article a clearly defined one; but I do not, and I think the gentlemen present will sustain me. The question was squarely asked, therefore, it ought to be squarely answered. Is the Lord's supper a sacrament or is it not? The word *rather* is sufficient to condemn any definition in the eyes of a philosopher. Take, for instance, the latter part of Article XXIX. To save my life I cannot tell whether the Lord's supper is a *sign* or a *sacrament:* 'But rather to their condemnation do eat and drink the sign or sacrament of so great a thing.' "

Father: "Rev. Gentlemen, let us keep cool. Our chat began pleasantly and it must end pleasantly. It is not necessary to go into details. If Bible readers cannot agree on so important a matter as the Lord's Supper, I think you have furnished sufficient proof that the Bible is not a good *Rule of Faith.* If you representative men disagree, you men of intelligence, what may we expect from the less intelligent, not to say from the ignorant, who are told that they alone are the judges of the Bible, though you preach to them and ask them to follow you. 'In 1527, Luther counted already no less than eight different interpretations of the text: *This is my body!* Thirty years afterwards there were no less than eighty-five!' (See Audin, p. 408, note.) By this time there must be many more."

Pastor: "Father, you are taking things rather easy. Permit us to put you on the defensive for awhile. What definition have you for the Lord's supper!"

Father. "Very well! I have one consolation. Mr. Knox may not accept our doctrine on this point, but he can not and will not object to the definition itself. It is plain and simple—every child can understand it. Here it is: 'The Holy Eucharist is the true body and the true blood of our Lord Jesus Christ, who is really and substantially present under the appearances of bread and wine for the nourishment of our souls.'"

Knox: "No objections can be raised to this definition."

Exhorter: "But this doctrine is unscriptural—we do not believe it."

Father: "Let us see—take the sixth chapter of the Gospel of St. John. Our Savior promises something better than manna: *I am the bread of life. Your fathers did eat manna in the desert, and they died.* The manna was an *extraordinary* bread. But, if what most of you say about the Lord's supper is true, it was inferior to manna.

Now, did the disciples understand the Savior, literally, as we Catholics do to-day?

'I am the living bread which came down from Heaven. If any man eat of this bread, he shall live forever; and the bread which I *will give, is my flesh* for the life of the world.' Had they not understood Him literally, it would have been nonsense, pure and simple, to raise the following objection: 'The Jews therefore debated (Prot. version, *strove*) among themselves, saying: How can this man give us his flesh to eat?' Had our Savior not meant what He said, He should have given the necessary explanations, as every honorable man will do when he sees he is misunderstood. But listen: *My flesh is meat indeed, and my blood is drink indeed.* This is a confirmation instead of a removal of the impression made. How did the disciples understand the Savior? Just as we Catholics do. 'Many, therefore, of his disciples hearing it, said: This saying is hard, and who can hear it? But Jesus, knowing in himself that His disciples murmured at this, said to them: Doth this scandalize you?' Surely, Mr. Knox's doctrine would not have scandalized the disciples. But what did they do? *After this many of his disciples went back, and walked no more with him.* Something extraordinary must have scared them off. It could not have been Zwingli's doctrine, for there is nothing scary about it. Did our Savior call them back and explain himself, as he should have done in case he was misunderstood? No. But He turns to the twelve and says: *Will you also go away?* Do *you* believe what I say? 'Simon Peter answered him: Lord, to whom shall we go? Thou hast the words of eternal life.' If the Jews do not believe you, if the disciples forsake you, we shall not abandon you, especially when you promise us so great a token of love.

However, this is only a promise, fulfilled on the eve of His passion and death: *Take ye and eat. This is my body.*

St. Paul, too, understood the Savior literally. 'But let a man prove himself, and so let him eat of that bread, and drink of the chalice. For he that eateth and drinketh unworthily, eateth and drinketh judgment, • (Prot. version, *damnation*) to himself, *not discerning the body of the Lord.*' Eating of common bread and drinking of ordinary wine can not be the cause of our *damnation.*

Of course, I could prove by the *Fathers* that our doctrine dates back to Christ and the Apostles. In the first place, our time is limited; in the second place, you may read the *Faith of Our Fathers* and all doubts will be removed."

Pastor: "It seems Luther was well aware of this, for he writes to the Christians at Strasburg: 'If five years ago Dr. Carlstadt, or anybody else, had been able to persuade me that there is nothing but bread and wine in the Sacrament, he would, I confess, have rendered me a great service. I have undergone severe struggles and *have twisted and turned to get over it*, because I was fully aware that it would have been the most severe blow which I could have dealt against Popery. * * * But I am in prison. I can not escape. The text (*This is my body*) is too powerful, and no words can make it mean anything else."

Exhorter: "I do not care a straw about Luther's opinion.   My senses say, it is bread and wine; therefore, it is bread and wine."

Father: When our Savior was baptized, a dove hovered over Him.   At least the senses said so; therefore, it was a dove!"

Knox: "I do not understand it; therefore, I do not believe it."

Father: "If you believe only what you understand, you have very little to believe.   Do you understand how the grass grows?   How a rotting acorn produces an immense oak?   If so, explain it at once."

Pastor: "I am ready to give up the floor.   The gentlemen may think that I have monopolized the grounds."

Father: "Of course, you have a right to give up the floor, but, in the meanwhile, I shall claim the victory.   I have shown that Luther was a bad man; that, by his example, he corrupted the morals of the people; that he changed the sacred text unscrupulously; that he taught new and unheard-of doctrines; that the Bible is not and cannot be the *Rule of Faith*, since we, representative men of large and intelligent Christian bodies, cannot and do not agree as to the most important doctrine—the Lord's supper.   Therefore, Luther was not a reformer; therefore, it is sinful to uphold him or his teachings."

II. EPISCOPALIAN.

Archdeacon: "My turn comes next. I am a defender of Henry VIII., styled by the Pope of Rome *Defensor fidei, i. e. Defender of the Faith.* Therefore Episcopalianism must be to the Father less objectionable than Lutheranism."

Father: "Please give us a short history of Henry."

Archdeacon: "Henry VIII. is a famous historical character. He was a contemporary of Dr. Martin Luther. He wrote a book against the German Reformers. He was a special friend of the reigning Pope, Clement VII., from whom he received his glorious title. You see, then, England's Reformer moved in good society. You may have shown that Luther was not God's chosen vessel to reform the Church, but I am glad to say Henry VIII. was not Luther."

Pastor: "Excuse me—one word only. If Luther was a bad man, Henry was not a whit better. Of course, I do not believe all the Father says. It is hard for him to overcome innate prejudices."

Father: "You must remember, my friend, that I have had very little to say; the Reformers spoke for me. By discrediting them you throw up the sponge. Either they told the truth about themselves or they did not; if they did, they were a set of bad men; if not, they were so nevertheless, for deceivers are not good. Therefore, I shall continue quoting reformer against reformer. No honest man can object to this mode of warfare.

I admit, Henry was once considered a good man, but many a good man has fallen from grace. Evidentyl, he did not keep good company when he married Anne Boleyn."

Archdeacon: "You surprise me, Father. No people hold Christian wedlock more sacred than you do. For this you command the respect of the world. Henry had married the good Catharine of Aragon, the widow of his deceased brother, Arthur. Having lived with her eighteen years, in 1527, his conscience began to trouble him seriously as to the validity of his marriage."

Exhorter: "Strange, indeed! Henry passed himself off for a theologian, and yet it took him eighteen years to find out whether he was lawfully married or not."

Father: "I thought so too. But let us hear Sir James Mackintosh: 'Whether Henry really felt any scruple respecting the validity of his marriage during the first eighteen years of his reign, may be reasonably doubted. No trace of such doubts can be discovered in his public conduct till the year 1527. * * * About the same time, Anne Boleyn, a damsel of the court, at the age of twenty-two, in the flower of youthful beauty, and full of graces and accomplishments, touched the fierce but not unsusceptible heart of the King. * * * The light which shone from Anne Boleyn's eyes might have awakened or revived Henry's doubts of the legitimacy of his long union with the faithful and blameless Catharine. His licentious passions, by a singular operation, recalled his mind to his theological studies, (History of England, p. 222, American Edit.) Listen to Agnes Strickland: 'Meantime, a treatise on the unlawfulness of his present marriage was compounded by the King and some of his favorite divines. How painfully and laboriously the royal theologian toiled in this literary labyrinth, is evinced by a letter written by himself to the fair lady, *whose bright eyes had afflicted him with such unwonted qualms of conscience.*' (Lives of the Queens of England, vol. IV, p. 142)."

Bro. Wesley: "Tell us something about Jane Seymour."

Father: "Love, purely carnal, is of short duration. Anne was accused of infidelity and treason. Her wretched life ended on the block. 'He had wept at the death of Catharine; but, as if to display his contempt for the memory of Anne, he dressed himself in white on the day of her execution, and was married to Jane Seymour next morning.' (Lingard, vol. IV, p. 250.) Says Agnes Strickland: "It is commonly asserted that he wore white for mourning the day after Anne Boleyn's execution; he certainly wore white, not as mourning, but because he on that day wedded her rival.' (Queens of England, vol. IV. p. 219)."

Exhorter: "Next in order would be Anne of Cleves."

Father: "She had the misfortune of being *homely*, therefore, she was divorced."

Mr. Knox: "Catharine Howard was also divorced."

Father: "And beheaded too. Henry's sixth and last wife, Catharine Parr, survived him, though she narrowly escaped death at his hands. Yet, by the English people, Henry VIII is looked upon as a reformer of the Church of God. The truth is, Henry had himself declared supreme head of the Church of England because the Pope refused to grant him the privilege of having more than one wife at a time. Says D'Israeli, in his Amenities of Literature (vol. I, p. 351): 'The policy was English, but it originated in the private passions of the monarch. Assuredly, had the tiara deigned to nod to the royal solicitor, then had the *Defender of the Faith* only given to the world another edition of his book against Luther.' Consequently, according to Protestant authorities, the Church of England was conceived in sin. In Buck's Theological Dictionary we read of Henry VIII: 'Falling out with the Pope about his marriage, he took the government of ecclesiastical affairs into his own hand, and having reformed many abuses, intitulated himself *supreme head* of the church.' 1 need not tell you that Buck is an inveterate enemy to the Catholic Church."

Archdeacon: "Remember, Father, we are Catholics, but not *Roman* Catholics."

Father: "I know you like to pose as Catholics. But, Rev. Gentlemen, I call on you at once to decide the question between the Archdeacon and myself. Suppose a stranger were to come to this town. At the depot he asks: Where does the Catholic clergyman live? Tell me: would any man in this wide world direct him to a *Protestant Episcopal* preacher? No, indeed. The world will never identify you as Catholics. It is a prerogative that the Roman Catholic alone enjoys by the common consent of the human family."

Exhorter: "But to come back to Henry's *supremacy*; I have often thought that he is an usurper as well as the Pope of Rome."

Father: "Usurpation consists in the appropriation of something not belonging to us. Either the Pope of Rome is the successor of St. Peter, or, he is not: if he is, what he claims belongs to him by divine right, as I have shown you, in my SHORT LINE TO THE ROMAN CATHOLIC CHURCH. I go one step further. The Pope is bound to claim what belongs to him in virtue of the words addressed to St. Peter, the first Pope. Were he not to do so, he would not only exhibit weakness, but he would shirk the performance of a duty put upon *his* shoulders, a duty which no other man can take upon himself without becoming an usurper. Of this we accuse Henry, in whom we have a full fledged, but self-constituted Pope. Prior to his time, who ever saw a layman in this capacity? Just think of it! A man who spends his time in divorcing and killing wives is declared by an act of Parliament the supreme head of the Church of England! The Pope refuses to grant his royal majesty a divorce, there fore he is forbidden the country which he had christianized. Talk about usurpation; here we have it in all its deformity. Let me. impress it on your mind: Henry VIII. was the first Pope, self-constituted Pope, of the Church of England, founded not by God, but *established by law*. What say you to this, Archdeacon?"

Archdeacon: "Henry was not so bad as he is generally supposed to be. You speak of a Church of England as a new institution. Remember, he did not make many changes in matters of faith."

Father: "The change of one single article of faith would suffice to condemn the whole concern. Our Savior says: *Teaching them to observe all things whatsoever I have commanded you.* Henry completely upset the government of the Church by having himself appointed its chief head.

"Either the Pope was appointed chief pastor in the

person of St. Peter, or he was not. In my SHORT
LINE I have shown you that he was: therefore, Henry
was an impostor. Furthermore, Edward VI. and *Good
Queen Bess* made more radical changes."

Bro. Wesley: "What objections have you to
Edward?"

Father: "When Henry died in 1547, Edward, the
son of *Jane Seymour*, being in his ninth year,
ascended the throne of England. This, of course,
made a boy *Pope*—a thing never heard of before.
The Reformation became more radical from day to
day. The Book ot Common Prayer was completed
for the time being; but what a transformation has it
not undergone!"

Archdeacon: "The truth is sometimes slow in
coming; at other times it comes with a rush."

Father: "Here we see the son reforming the doc-
trinal work of the father; we see a Pope against a
Pope; every dày some doctrines are thrown over-
board and new ones made to order. If the people in
time of the father had the true faith, they are surely
robbed of it now; if they enjoyed this blessing in the
time of the son, they evidently believed in false doctrines during the father's reign. Therefore, the
Episcopalian Church has been false since its separation from Rome. If so, it may be false now. This is
admitted by the Rev. William R. Huntington, D. D.,
Rector of Grace Church, New York City: 'Take the
Christian people of this land in the mass, it is probably true of its several divisions that no one of them
is entirely in the right upon all points, and no one of
them upon all points entirely in the wrong. It is
clearly desirable that those who are more in the right

and less in the wrong than others should come to the
front; but which these are can be known, only by the
test of time. God, by some sifting process of His
own, will ultimately sever the evil from the good and
manifest His Church.' (*Why I Am What I Am*, pp.
45-46). Just think of it! According to this testimony, we are still groping in the dark. It will soon
be 2,000 years since our blessed Lord established His
Church, against which the gates of hell should not
prevail, and which he promised to be with to the
end of time. One Reformer after another has come
to the front since the sixteenth century; yet we are
told, in this nineteenth century, by an eminent
divine, a representative man of the Protestant Episcopal Church, a New Yorker too, that we are only
guessing at the truth; that, in other words, to this
day the truth is hidden from our view, that sooner or
later, it is sincerely hoped, God in His mercy by *some
sifting process*, will let us know what to do and believe to save our immortal souls. Gentlemen, what
have you to say in reply?"

Exhorter: "It is heart-rending, indeed, to a lover
of souls. This New Yorker ought to be retired at
once. He has no settled convictions."

Archdeacon: "Our convictions are settled; we do
not depend on a certain man in New York. Look at
our Book of Common Prayer, issued in the reign of
Edward VI, whom the Father is pleased to call Pope
of England."

Father: "I beg your pardon, this book has undergone so many changes that it is almost impossible
to keep track of them. On this subject read Bishop
Short, p. 278. It will surprise you. Read also *His*

Majesty's Declaration in the *Convocation holden at London in the year 1562.* You will find it in the *Book of Common Prayer,* printed and published at London by A. J. Valpy, M. A., p. 493.   I have it before me just now.   In this declaration His Majesty more than once tells his subjects, that he is the 'Supreme Governor of the Church of England'; that its *Articles* are to be received unconditionally; 'that no man hereafter shall either print or preach, to draw the Article aside any way, but shall submit to it in the plain and full meaning thereof; and shall not put his *own sense* or comment to be the meaning of the Article, but shall take it in the literal and grammatical sense,' that the offenders 'shall be liable to *our displeasure*' * * * 'And we will see there shall be due execution upon them.' This almost forbids a man to *think.* Talk about liberty of conscience! Rome never has been nor could be more stringent.

Archdeacon :   "But the Thirty-nine Articles are good, very good.   There is nothing more to the point than they are."

Father :   Let us examine a few of them.   Remember the *Side-Switches* ought not be so long as the *Main Line,* known as the SHORT LINE TO THE ROMAN CATHOLIC CHURCH. In other words, the portico ought never be larger than the house   But, to the point; of what does the sixth article treat?"

Archdeacon : "I know the Thirty-nine Articles by heart.   It treats of the *Sufficiency of the Holy Scriptures for Salvation.*"

Father : "Our dissension on the Lord's supper proves its *insufficiency.* Therefore this article falls to the ground. No power on earth could induce you five representative men to worship in the same church every Sunday in the year. Why? The Bible is not *sufficient* to make you agree on matters pertaining to salvation. This article is a powerful lever in the hands of infidels. It ought to put us to shame when we have to face them. This *sufficiency* is a hot-bed of infidelity.

Furthermore, the article in question tells us that in the Old Testament twenty-four books are positively to be received, whereas fourteen may be 'Read for example of life and instruction of manners.'

Suppose I were to object to this wholesale throwing over-board, as we Catholics, forming the greatest body of Christians on earth, actually do, are the Scriptures *alone sufficient* to convince me what must be accepted or rejected? Gentlemen, this article bears on its brow the stamp of impracticability and falsehood—it ought to be wiped out of the Book of Common Prayer, to prevent a common sense infidel from laying his eyes on it.

Archdeacon : These things must be taken *cum grano salis*, especially when we read in Article XI : 'We are justified by faith only.' ''

Father: ''For a full refutation of this article, read *Catholic Belief.* But from it let me quote : 'Suppose a man afflicted with a grave disease sends for a physician of repute. The physician comes and prescribes, and, to inspire the patient with more confidence, tells him : *Only believe in me and you will be cured.* Can we suppose that the poor sufferer, on the departure of the physician, would say : *I shall take no medicine, for the physician said: Only believe and you will be cured?"* "

Archdeacon : "According to the Article XIX, we need not look for perfection in this world, for we read : 'As the Church of Jerusalem, Alexandria and Antioch have erred, not only in their living and manner of Ceremonies, but also in matters of Faith——' "

Father : Do the people at large of your Church know this article?"

Archdeacon : "Indeed, they do.   It is in the Book of Common Prayer."

Father : "It is surprising that you have any following whatever.   Were we to say to our people : 'We are or we may be in the wrong,' they would— and I believe consistently—either abandon the Church before sunrise or hurl into our teeth the words of Christ : *The gates of hell shall not prevail against it.* They would say :   Christ is not and cannot be a liar. It is blasphemous to think so and more blasphemous to say so."

Archdeacon : "You Catholics make too much of Church authority.   It is true, Article XIX upholds it too, but it also adds : 'Yet it is not lawful for the Church to ordain anything that is contrary to God's word written.'   And in the following article we read : 'General Councils * * * may err, and sometimes have erred, even in things pertaining to God.   Wherefore, things ordained by them as necessary to salvation have neither strength nor authority, unless it may be declared that they be taken out of Holy Scripture.' "

Father: "What a bundle of doubts—thank God I have never been in this labyrinth! Episcopalians, who have the salvation of their souls at heart, must occasionally be very miserable. You are bound to admit that the Church is older than the Bible, as we have it. If it is, why should the Bible supersede it? If it has at a later period done so, please tell me when, where, and by whose authority. According to the statement just made, you have more confidence in type-setters, proof-readers, folders and binders than in General Councils of the Church of England. Even if the latter could make mistakes, why not the former? At least, we have every reason to believe a General Council more scrupulous than a union type-setter, who is liable to be a professed infidel."

Bro. Wesley: "The Article XXXIII. speaks of excommunication. Father, practically, at least from your standpoint, this would be nonsense, pure and simple.

Father: "Indeed, it would. If the Bible be the Rule of Faith and if its interpretation depend on the individual, how can excommunication affect him? One may excommunicate the other, but the one does no harm to the other. These excommunications are no *thunderbolts*."

Exhorter: "Bro. Wesley, Article XXXII. speaks of the *Marriage of Priests*. You passed over it, but I should like to know why Catholic priests do not marry? Of course, I mean the Roman priests. Father, does your Church consider it forbidden by the law of God.'"

Father: "Not at all, sir; we look upon celibacy as a matter of expediency. We believe with St.

Paul, that a married man 'is solicitous for the things of this world, how he may please his wife; and he is divided.' A married priest would be like a married soldier—half a soldier. In the nature of things a married priest would pay more attention to the wants of his wife and children than to the welfare of his congregation. Furthermore, the great Apostle says, it is *better* not to marry."

Archdeacon: "We admit, St. Paul says so; but God himself says, *increase and multiply.*"

Father: "Either the Apostle of the Gentiles is an inspired writer, or he is not. If he is, he cannot come in conflict with God. Therefore, the words *increase and multiply* do not imply that every individual is in conscience bound to marry. If he were, he should also be told at what age and on what date this duty devolves upon him. The insane, the sick and infirm should be compelled to comply with this obligation; it would necessitate an equal number of males and females, not to speak of those unfortunate ladies who are forever on the alert, but have no *chance.*"

Knox: "I do not believe any one should be forced to lead a life of celibacy."

Father: "You are right; we believe so too. Therefore we do not force a man to become a priest. We could not do so even if we wished. Therefore, no man is forbidden to marry. The Church only says to the aspirant, this is the *conditio sine qua non*— that is, indispensable to the state of life you embrace.'"

Exhorter: "If all were to do what St. Paul considers *better*, the world would soon die out."

Father: "Let us not borrow trouble; there is no immediate danger of the whole world doing *better*."

Bro. Wesley: "The American Edition seems to be more *manly* than the English!"

Father: "You are right, Bro. Wesley. But, remember, some one is doing the *thinking* for our Episcopalian brethren."

Exhorter: "*Sapienti sat*, no more about the *Prayer Book*. Speaking of Elizabeth, I think she was a good women—*Good Queen Bess.*"

Father: The Protestant writers, Hallam, Miss Strickland, Macaulay, not to mention our own Prescott, do not always agree with you. Read them and be convinced to the contrary. I shall only call your attention to the murder of poor Mary, Queen of Scots."

Knox: "Your time is up, Archdeacon. Give Presbyterians a chance."

Father: "I am satisfied; but, either I have shown that some of the Thirty-nine Articles are nonsensical, and that Protestant authorities consider the reformers of the Church of England bad fellows, or I have not done so. If I have, the Archdeacon ought to be forced to admit it."

III. THE PRESBYTERIAN SIDE-SWITCH.

Archdeacon : "Take the floor, Mr. Knox."

Father: "Who is the founder of the Presbyterian Church?"

Knox: "Jesus Christ, of course. Who could think of anybody else?"

Father : "The reason I ask the question is this: Both the Pastor and the Archdeacon claim that Christ is the founder of their respective Churches. Since these Churches contradict each other, and since Christ can not contradict himself, reason and common sense tell us Catholics that the Savior can not be the founder of all. Furthermore, history records no Presbyterian Church prior to the Reformation."

Knox: "You see, Father, the Church of Rome became very corrupt. God, in his mercy, sent John Calvin, born at Nogen, in Picardy, A. D. 1509, to purify it. This, by the way, was a great undertaking, but Calvin was equal to the task.

"Calvinism having been established at Geneva, it was transplanted by my name-sake, John Knox, into Scotland, where Presbyterianism has a strong foothold. I am willing to admit with the Presbyterian, Charles Seymour Robinson, D.D., New York: 'The system of faith that we cherish is Calvinism, but we do not cherish it because John Calvin originated it.' (*Why I Am What I Am.*)

Exhorter: "If he originated it, he surely must be the founder of it."

Father: "I think so, too. But, let us pass over this. I notice Presbyterians are divided. We have English Presbyterians, Presbyterians in the United States, Cumberland Presbyterians and the Reformed Presbytery. Tell me, where shall I look for the truth? When two contradict each other, both may be in the wrong, but one must necessarily be so."

Knox: "For my part I prefer those who style themselves 'Presbyterians in the United States.' No man ought to go back on his own country. I do not believe in foreigners dictating to our consciences."

Father: "According to your principle, the Romans should not have accepted the Christian religion at the hands of St. Peter, a foreigner. As to the Cumberland Presbyterians, they are also in the United States. To save time, however, I am willing to pass over these questions, which may seem indifferent to you, whereas we look upon them as a matter of great importance. What reasons have you to prefer your Church to the Lutheran, Episcopalian or any other?"

Knox: "Let me quote the Rev. Chas. S. Robinson again: 'The one peerless pecularity of this creed of ours is found in the fact that the whole of it is framed absolutely upon the word of God.' In this the Rev. Gentleman agrees with the Confession of Faith, p. 8: 'The authority of the Holy Scripture, for which it ought to be believed and obeyed, dependeth not upon the testimony of any man or church, but wholly upon God, the author thereof, and therefore it is to be received, because it is the word of God.'"

Pastor: "I object to this. It is no distinctive *peculiarity*. We Lutherans believe the very same thing."

Archdeacon: "So do we—read Article VI."

Bro. Wesley: "The world believes it, except perhaps, the Father."

Father: "Right or wrong, Bro. Wesley. I do not believe it, nor does the *world*, if by *world* we understand the majority of Christians. What is still better, Mr. Knox does not believe it himself. It he does, he must come in conflict with Article VIII., p. 12, which, after telling us in what languages the Scriptures were written, says: 'But because these original tongues are not known to all the people of God who have right unto, and interest in the Scriptures, and are commanded in the fear of God, to read and search them, therefore they are to be translated into the vulgar language of *every nation*.' This is a task; a work of gigantic proportions, and, it seems to me, the testimony of a great *many men* must be taken into consideration. However, let us consider the work of one only; I mean the translator's. In the first place, he would have to be a good man, for a bad man might corrupt the Scriptures. In the second place, he would have to be free from all prejudices; but even good men are often subject to them. For instance, we all admit that our friend, the Exhorter, is a good man. But if he were to translate from the original text, I fear he would emphasize the word *immersion* quite frequently."

Knox: "I would not let him do so."

Father: "Whose testimony should we take into consideration, yours or his? But Article IV. says: 'The authority of the Holy Scripture * * * dependeth not upon the testimony of *any man*.' In the third place, since the meaning of words changes, the translator would have to be a very wise man; he would have to know the full import of words used 2,000 or 3,000 years ago. You set infallibility aside; therefore nothing remains but a *bundle of doubts*."

Archdeacon: "Catholics are inveterate enemies of the Bible."

Father: "Not at all, sir. If we are in the wrong, point out the errors. We are open to conviction, but we shall always object to inconsistencies."

Pastor: "Introduce some other subject, Mr. Knox, the Bible question is getting monotonous."

Knox: "Again I quote our representative man in New York: 'Let me put with this another character-istic of Presbyterian preference. We consider doc-trine as the one peculiarity of the church. We exalt dogma above everything else, whether of polity or history.' "

Father: "The New York gentleman seems to de-light in contradictions. In *Why I Am What I Am*, p. 25, he says the contrary: 'Pastors exchange pul-pits without hesitation with every Christian denomi-nation without exception. Seven or eight of the chief churches of our name here in the City of New York called their pastors directly from other com-munions, and nobody interposed objections.' "

Bro. Wesley: "This is a loose way of handling *dogmas*. Look here, Mr. Knox, if you wish to con-quer the Father, drop the New Yorker. Take up your Confession of Faith and talk to him about pre-destination. Other denominations may be inoculated with it, but it surely is a Presbyterian characteristic.

Knox: "Very well. 'By the decree of God, for the manifestation of his glory, some men and angels are predestinated into life everlasting, and others fore-ordained to everlasting death. These angels and men, thus predestinated and fore-ordained, are particularly and unchangeably designed, and their number is so certain and definite that it cannot be either increased or diminished Those of mankind that are predestinated unto life, God, before the foundation of the world was laid * * * hath chosen in Christ unto everlasting glory, out of his mere free grace and love, without any foresight of faith or good works, or perseverance in either of them, or any other thing in. the creature, as conditions or causes moving him thereto, and all to the praise of his glorious grace.' (pp. 23-24.)"

Father: "What has your Confession of Faith to say about the heathens? Suppose they try to live according to the law of nature inscribed in their hearts; that they use all means at their command to save themselves; that they are most heartily sorry for sins committed, and they are fully determined to sin no more?"

Knox: "Our doctrine is well defined. See Article IV., p. 65. 'Others, not elected, * * * much less can men, not professing the Christian religion, be saved in any other way whatsoever, be they never so diligent to frame their lives according to the light of nature, and the law of that religion they do profess; and to maintain that they may is very pernicious and to be detested.'"

Exhorter: "We believe all children go to heaven."

Knox: "We believe this of the elect only. 'Elect infants, dying in infancy, are regenerated and saved by Christ through the Spirit * * * So also are all other elect persons, who are incapable of being outwardly called by the ministry of the word.'"

Archdeacon: Indeed, the terms used by the Presbyterians are unmistakable in their meaning."

Pastor: "Yes, but this iron-clad predestination is, after all, horrible."

Father: "The Catholic Church abhors it. *It blights every hope.* For instance, Mr. Knox, if your child were to die you could not console yourself by saying it is in heaven; for you do not know whether it belongs to the elect or not. A Presbyterian mother, kneeling by the side of her darling's coffin, has every reason to be heart-broken. She herself may belong to the elect, whereas her loved one may be inscribed in the book of the non-elect, which means damnation—everlasting separation from God and mother.

Practically, it is a death blow to every good thought. 'Works done by unregenerated men * * * are therefore, sinful and cannot please God, or make a man meet to receive grace from God. And yet their neglect of them is more sinful and displeasing unto God.' P. 89. In other words, you sin if you do; and you sin if you don't.

It fosters vice. 'They whom God has accepted in His beloved * * * can neither totally nor finally fall away from the state of grace; but shall certainly persevere therein to the end, and be eternally saved.' P. 91.

It robs man of his free will. 'This perseverance of the saints depends not upon their own free will, but upon the immutability of the decree of election.' Ibid."

Knox: "Bear in mind, Father, our Church is progressive. You must have noticed in the papers that we are on the eve of making a change in the Confession of Faith, and consequently our religious convictions should be treated with due respect."

Pastor: "The sooner the better, for such doctrine

will never stand the test of reason. In our own day the people are too enlightened."

Father: "It seems Mr. Knox admits his church has taught false doctrines in the past. If so, it may do the same thing in the future; therefore, it is dangerous to entrust one's salvation to this soul-trap. Just think of it, for more than 300 years the Presbyterians taught and believed something that God abhors; for, being the God of truth, He must hate falsehood."

Pastor: "Father, on this point I agree with you. From the beginning, the Lutherans objected to the Calvinistic doctrine: 'This opinion ought everywhere to be held in honor and execration; it is stoical madness, fatal to morals, monstrous and blasphemous.'" (*Corpus Doctrinæ Christianæ.*)

Father: "Calvin made a bad impression on his co-reformers. Erasmus pointing at young Calvin, said to Bucer: 'I see a great plague rising in the Church against the Church.' (*Video magnam pestem oriri in Ecclesia contra Ecclesiam*). On the other hand Bucer said: 'Calvin is a true mad dog. The man is wicked, and he judges of the people according as he loves or hates them.'"

Bro. Wesley: "If the founder has been wicked, and if the church has been false, let us lose no time on account of it. It is growing late; therefore, let us hear what the Exhorter has to say concerning the Baptist Church."

IV. BAPTIST SIDE-SWITCH.

Father: "I notice, Exhorter, the Baptists, like all other Protestants, are divided among themselves. We have the *Anti-pædobaptists* and the *Pædobaptists*. The former hold that adults *alone* are proper subjects for baptism, whereas the latter teach that children *too* may be baptized. To what class do you belong?"

Exhorter: "To the former, of course. I never heard of *Pædobaptists*."

Father: "Well, I saw the distinction in *Buck's Theological Dictionary*, a work extremely anti-Catholic. Therefore I referred to it. In an argument, the principal thing is to know what we are talking about. You will admit, however, the Baptists are not all of one mind. Of the subdivisions let me mention the following: *Anabaptists, Baptists, Christians, Disciples of Christ, Ephrata Baptists, Free-Will Baptists, Melchites, Seventh-Day Baptists, Six Principle Baptists* and *Dunkers*. I believe there are more; but, for all practical purposes, these ten species will suffice. Now, tell me, with what denomination do you claim fellowship? To ask you whether you consider them all in the right would be to insult your intelligence. To say that all are right would not even be *liberal*. We must never be liberal at the expense of reason. Of these denominations one does not consider the other in the right, hence the split."

Bro. Wesley: "Come out with it, Exhorter. *An open confession is good for the soul.*"

Exhorter: "I belong to the *Baptists*, represented by Rev. R. S. MacArthur, D. D., Pastor of Calvary Baptist Church, New York, in *Why I Am What I Am*, quoted so often by you with pleasure."

"Father: "Nothing like bringing the matter nearer home. Tell me, now, who is the founder of your church? We have seen that Luther is the father of Lutheranism; Henry VIII., or rather Elizabeth, of Episcopalianism; and Calvin, of Presbyterianism. But who inaugurated the Baptist sect as a Protestant Side-switch."

Exhorter: "Stop right there; it must be clearly understood that we are not Protestants."

Knox: "This will never do to tell. The Father does not consider you *Catholics*, and we always did look upon you as Protestants."

Exhorter: "Say what you please, I am neither a Roman Catholic nor a Protestant. My church dates back to St. John the Baptist. If you wish, you may call him the founder."

Bro. Wesley: "If there is anything in the world that Catholics always harp on, it is the age of their church. It takes the Exhorter to put them in the shade."

Father: "No objection whatever. Our religion comes from Christ, and we want no other founder under any consideration."

Exhorter: "You misunderstood me, Father. St. John the Baptist is only so far the founder of our church that he was the first to administer Baptism according to our mode. Really, Christ is the founder."

Father:. "Let's see if he is, my friend. I need not tell you that the Catholic church has an unbroken history—look back at her long line of Popes, from Leo XIII to St. Peter. In fact, the history of the church is so interwoven with world's history, that you cannot read the one without learning a deal about the other. Read any historian; either he speaks for or against the Popes and Bishops of the church. Be this as it may, he is bound to acknowledge their presence at any given time since the coming of Christ. Can this be said of the Baptist persuasion? If so, it is entitled to some consideration."

Exhorter: "Of course, it can. You will admit without proof, that the organization exists to-day. I need not remind you that our religion was introduced into this country at Providence, Rhode Island, in 1638, by Roger Williams and John Clark."

Father: "No man will deny these facts. Do not forget, however, Christ came into this world very nearly 1900 years ago."

Exhorter: "In the life-time of the Prince of Orange, the founder of the Dutch Republic, they were sometimes called Anabaptists—Rebaptizers."

Father: "Among historians the Anabaptists are not in very good odor. I am astonished that you dare call my attention to them at all. The city of Munster, Westphalia, was greatly disturbed by them in 1533, in the person of an inn-keeper, John Bockelson, famous as John of Leyden, and an executioner, Knipper Dolling. I shall quote no Catholic against this sect. But Vincent L. Wilner, in his *Religious Denominations of the world,*' calls them a *small party of fanatics in Munster.* Buck, the inveterate enemy of he Catholic Church, says of them in his *Theological Dictionary*, among other very bad things: * * * 'As neither the laws of nature nor the precepts of the New Testament had forbidden polygamy, they should use the same liberty as the patriarchs did in this respect.' " p. 15.

Knox: "Pass over the Anabaptists; you surely can refer us to something better."

Exhorter: "The Wickliffites were Baptists. John Wickliff was born in 1324 at Yorkshire. He bears the title of *first Reformer*."

Knox: "Look here, we claim John Wickliff.",

Father: "You are right, Mr. Knox. He 'thought the Pope was no longer the head of the church militant; there was no longer any use for cardinals, patriarchs, bishops and councils; the priests and deacons could discharge all the sacred functions.' Furthermore, he was a Catholic theologian at Oxford. Having been removed from the guardianship of the university he rebelled. If he did become a Baptist, it was wounded pride that made him take the step."

Pastor: "Try the Waldenses."

Exhorter: "They are said to have handed down the Baptist doctrine. Peter Waldo was a merchant of Lyons in 1160."

"Father: "In 1839, Mgr. Charvaz published the *Historical inquiries into the true origin of the Waldenses and into the nature of their primitive doctrine.* Let me call your attention to one or two of their doctrines: 1. Laymen can hear the confessions of the faithful and consecrate the Eucharist. 2. Not only men, but also women have the priestly power. 3. Divorce is lawful under all circumstances. Tell me, do you believe in these articles?"

Exhorter: "No, indeed."

Father: "Consequently, these Frankish heretics were not your forefathers in the faith. Therefore, you cannot claim them as a link in your chain to connect you with the first ages. If, however, you do, you must confess that your denomination has undergone changes. This would leave your church without a history of its own, since it can not be traced back to Christ and His Apostles. Even Buck, who sees something good in everybody except a Catholic, tells us that they 'prohibited and condemned in their society all wars and writs of law, and all attempts towards the acquisition of wealth; the inflicting of capital punishments, self-defense against unjust violence, and oaths of all kinds.' All these things are considered lawful to-day by all civilized nations of the globe."

Pastor: "I always did look upon the Waldenses as Socialists and Anarchists."

Father: "In the *History of the Reformed Church of Netherlands*, by Drs. Ypeig and Dermont, published in Breda in 1819, we read: 'We have now seen that the Baptists, who were formerly called Anabaptists, and in later times Mennonites, were the original Waldenses, and have long in the history of the church received the honor of that origin.' "

Bro. Wesley: "I do not wish to have a share in this honor."

Knox: "Who are the Mennonites?"

Father: "Let Buck speak again: 'A sect in the United Provinces, in most respects the same with

those in other places called Anabaptists. They had
their rise in 1536, when Menno Simon, a native of
Friesland, who had been a Romish priest and a noto-
rious profligate, resigned his rank and office in the
Romish Church, and publicly embraced the communion of the Anabaptists.'"

Bro. Wesley: "It seems many of the reformers
were bad Catholic priests."

Father: "Just so, Bro. Wesley. Some, thrown
overboard by excommunication, became leaders of
sects."

Archdeacon: "I presume it would be quite a task
to trace the Baptist Church back to Christ and the
Apostles. Many links seem to be missing."

Exhorter: "But the Father ought to know that
the Catholic Church herself administered Baptism
by immersion for more than a thousand years."

Knox: "He does know it. Therefore he raises no
objection to immersion itself; do you, Father?"

"Father: "Not at all, sir. As to its validity, it is
fully as effective as pouring. However, in the case of
infants, the sick and the dying, Baptism by immersion is very impractical, not to speak of the impro-
priety in the case of females."

Exhorter: "Father, you are caught now. The
sick, the dying and especially the children, who cannot believe, need no baptism. *He that believeth and
is baptized shall be saved.*"

Father: "How many years, months and days old
must the subject be when Baptism becomes necessary?"

Exhorter: "Baptism is not essential to salvation.
Let me quote from the Rev. R. S. MacArthur, D. D.:

'A Christian should, of course, be baptized as a soldier should put on a uniform; but as it is not putting on the uniform which makes a man a soldier, so it is not baptism that makes a man a Christian. The man puts on the uniform because he is already a soldier; and so a man should be baptized when he becomes a Christian.' * * * Another statement of the Baptist principle is this: 'Baptism is not necessary to salvation. The assertion sometimes made, that Baptists hold that no man can be saved unless he is baptized, is the falsest, absurdest, most idiotic declaration that ever was made in ecclesiastical controversy. It is difficult to speak with courtesy of such ignorance or malice. The very reason why Baptists practice baptism and not some substitute for it, such as pouring or sprinkling, is the fact that they hold that baptism is in no way essential to salvation. * * * The doctrine that all dying in infancy are saved was first taught by the Baptists. They held not only that an adult believer would be saved, though he died without baptism, but that all dying in infancy were saved. This doctrine continually appears in the charges against Baptists who were put to death for their faith. For instance, Henry Craut, Justus Mueller and John Peisker were beheaded at Jena in 1536, not by Roman Catholics but by their Protestant brethren, the Lutherans. Among their announced views was the doctrine that "all infants, even those of Turks, Gentiles and Hebrews, are saved without baptism." The first time this doctrine appears in a non-Baptist creed it is mentioned only to be condemned. The Augsburg Confession of 1530 says: "Damnant Anabaptistas, qui improbant baptismum puerorum et affirmant pueros sine baptismo salvos fieri " "They (the churches putting forth this creed) condemn the Anabaptists (a nickname of the Baptists) who reject the baptism of children and declare that children are saved without baptism.' (*Why I Am What I Am.*) "

Father: "I have the whole book from which you quote, before me. I sent for it especially. First, to

get the history of the Baptist Church; second, to
learn what articles of faith are taught.   To my surprise, however, I find in the long-winded article nothing but this, no proof, of course, being given: First,
children are saved without Baptism; second, adults
need not be baptized and the Baptist Church never
persecuted.   I ask you in the name of common sense,
what can a man learn from this book?   And yet the
article comes from the pen of a New York preacher,
whose capacity as a minister is certified by his position as a representative.   The only thing that Baptists harp on from January 1 to December 31 is Baptism, and this. they tell us, is not necessary.   What,
then, do they believe?   What is essential to salvation?"

Archdeacon: "Cut this debate short—it is growing
very late—it is a waste of time to talk about a church
devoid of history and articles of faith.   Bro. Wesley,
have you any remarks to make?"

V. BRO. WESLEY'S PLEA FOR RECOGNITION.

Bro. Wesley: "Late or not late, I insist on my rights; I, too, have something to say. You must bear in mind that the M. E. Church embraces the largest body of Christians in the United States."

Pastor: "It is true; the Methodists are very numerous in this country."

Father: "True and not true—just as you take it."

Bro. Wesley: "Explain yourself, father."

Father; There are so many *branches* of the Methodist family:

1. *The Welsh Calvinistic Methodists*, founded by Howel Harris, a companion of Wesley and Whitfield. They principally exist in Wales.

2. *The Countess of Huntingdon's Connection.*

3. *The Methodist New Connection*, formed in 1797.

4. *The Band Room Methodists* had their origin in Manchester in 1806. They are now called, '*The United Free Gospel Churches.*'

5. *The Primitive Methodists*; Staffordshire, 1810.

6. *The Bible Christians*, sometimes called 'Bryanites,' were founded by William C. Bryan, a Wesleyan local preacher, in Cornwall, in 1815.

7. *The Primitive Methodists in Ireland*, receded from the parent body in 1817.

8. *The United Methodist Free Churches* are an amalgamation of three different splits from the original connection.

9. *The Wesleyan Reform Union*, 1849.

10. *The Congregational Methodists.*
11. *Methodist Protestants.*
12. *Methodist Society.*
13. *Reformed Methodists.*
14. *Wesleyan Methodists.*
15. *Colored Methodist Episcopal.*
16. *Methodist Episcopal Church."*

Exhorter: "I move that we adjourn. It would take weeks to bring order out of this chaos. By the way, Father, where did you get all this information about *Methodism?"*

Father: "Not to speak of *Disciplines,* I have Buck's *Theological Dictionary,* Religious *Denominations of the World,* Life and *Times of John Wesley,* by L· Tyerman, in three volumes, 1,881 pages; and last but not least, *Why I Am What I Am,* for it gives us modern Methodism. But, as the Exhorter well remarked, it would take too long to examine all the branches of the Methodist family; therefore we shall confine ourselves to yours, Bro. Wesley. Tell us which one it is of the sixteen enumerated."

Bro. Wesley: "I represent the M. E. Church. The Methodist denomination 'was founded in the year 1729, by one Mr. Morgan and Mr. John Wesley,' my name-sake. They were soon joined by Charles Wesley and the renowned Whitfield. In 1735 John and Charles Wesley, accompanied by a few others, came to Georgia to preach the Gospel to the benighted Indians of our great country. 'After Mr. Whitfield returned from America in 1741, he declared his full assent to the doctrines of Calvin. Mr. Wesley, on the contrary, professed the Arminian doctrine, and had written in favor of perfection and universal redemption, and very strongly against election, (a doctrine) which Mr. Whitfield believed to be scriptural. The difference, therefore, of sentiments between these two great men caused a separation.' (Buck's Theol. Dict). What objections have you to raise against this, gentlemen?"

All: "They had a right to their *contrary* opinions. Father, what have you to say?"

Father: "It does not and would not satisfy a Catholic theologian, for the following reasons:

1.   To him the very idea of establishing a church 1729 years *after* Christ, seems perfectly ridiculous. We believe in Christ: *The gates of hell shall not prevail against* the church. It seems, Bro. Wesley puts his whole faith and trust in the Wesley Brothers. With us it is 'Jesus Christ, yesterday and to-day, and the same forever.'   Heb. 13-8.

2.   Either the Methodist church was solidly founded in 1729, or it was not; if it was, it seems strange that it began to tumble down only 12 years later, in 1741. *I will be with you all days, even to the consummation of the world.* You see, we Catholics have implicit confidence in the *word of God.* On the other hand, it seems you have none at all. Thanks be to God for the faith that is in us!

3.   The difference between the Calvinistic and Arminian doctrine is as great as the difference between day and night; yes, heaven and hell. Yet it is looked upon as a mere matter of *sentiment* between *two great men.* Surely, they considered something more than a *sentiment;* if not, they were *little* men indeed. But, go on, Bro. Wesley."

Bro. Wesley: "The first Methodist society in the United States was formed in the city of New York, in 1766, by a few Methodist emigrants from Ireland: The political revolutiȯ of 1776 brought about many changes and *led to the formal organization* and establishment of The Methodist Episcopal Church, of which I have the honor of being a member. In 1784, Dr. Thomas Coke came to America with powers to constitute Methodist societies into an *independent* church in the United States. He ordained Francis Asbury bishop; for, 'hitherto the societies had been dependent on *other* churches for the ordinances of baptism and the Lord's supper, as the Methodist preachers were considered only lay-preachers, and according to the uniform advice of Mr. Wesley, had declined administering the ordinances.'" (Buck's Theol. Dict.)

Father: "Worse and worse. Either ordination was necessary, or it was not; if it was, the M. E. Church dates back no farther than 1784. Therefore it is a new thing—a little more than 100 years old--it is an innovation--it does not come from Christ and the Apostles.

The Wesley Brothers themselves never intended to sever connection with the *Established Church of England*.

Archdeacon: "We always did look upon the M. E. Church as an off-shoot of Episcopalianism."

Father: "You are right, Archdeacon. It is this and nothing more. If, however, as we have seen, the church *established* by *law* cannot be traced back further than Henry VIII, it follows that Methodism is out of the race altogether. But, do tell us, Bro. Wesley, why are you a Methodist Episcopalian?"

Bro. Wesley: "Let me quote the Rev. George W. McGrew:

It is, I suppose, easy to mistake *bigness for greatness;* and few men would now claim that Providence is on the side of the heaviest battalions. But to those who believe in Christ's providential guidance of His Church, the unprecedented growth of Methodism, apart from other indications, constitutes an implied divine sanction of the movement. Still I think that if I were an Englishman, resident in England to-day, I should be a Churchman rather than a Wesleyan. But since I am an American, the same considerations which would then lead me to adopt the one course now impel me to be a member of the Methodist Episcopal Church. An enumeration of these considerations must be my answer to the question, Why I am a Methodist Episcopalian? rather than a Protestant Christian of some other name. (Why I am what I am.) "

Pastor: "Mohametamism spread much faster than Methodism, but no one considers the fact as a proof of *providential guidance.*"

Exhorter: "The M. E. Church is pre-eminently an American institution. This is admitted on all hands. Since Christ is the author of the *Christian* religion, I prefer it to an American one.

Father: "A man that would change his religion, whenever he moves to another country, has no settled convictions—no religion at all—he is a *turn-coat.* In the eyes of all thinking, intelligent and honest people, he must be an object of pity."

Bro. Wesley: "Gentlemen, condemn no man without a hearing. Mr. McGrew gives reasons for the *faith that is in him.* He says he belongs to the M. E. Church, *because it is a church. It is a branch of that divine society which Christ said he would build.*

Pastor: "It seems you are satisfied with a *branch* of the truth.   Our Savior says: *Teaching them to observe* ALL THINGS, *whatsoever I have commanded you.*"

Father: "But look at the other point.   He is a member of the M. E. Church because it is A church. Evidently the gentleman believes in more than one church.   He believes that Christ can contradict himself by establishing conflicting churches.   *Upon this rock I will build* MY *church*, not churches.   The men of thought in his audience are to be pitied."

Bro. Wesley: "Says Mr. Grew, 'In the next place ours is an Episcopal Church.   It is not a Presbyterian or a Congregational Church.' "

Knox: "I do not believe in Episcopacy."

. Father: "Mr. McGrew himself doubts it, for he adds, p. 29: 'The irregularity in the manner of securing the succession from the English Church is cured in the same way that numerous irregularities were covered during the Reformation in England iu the seventeenth century.   What the judicious Hooker called the *exigence of necessity*.' It seems Mr. Hooker believed in the transmission of Apostolic powers. Either the Apostolic succession is necessary or it is not; if it is, the *exigence of necessity* will not supply the missing link, for *nemo dat quod non habet*—no man can give what he hasn't got.   Therefore, *irregularities* make your Episcopacy null and void; therefore, you boast of something you have not received.   If Protestants had thrown the *Apostolic succession* overboard, they would have fared better.   I admit, however, it is hard to discard truth altogether; it will cling to us in spite of us.   Therefore we try to retain the appearance it we cannot lay our hands on the reality.   Bu

Mr. McGrew's admission is a source of satisfaction to us; it proves that others would like to have what we possess.''

Archdeacon: "The Rev. gentleman gave himself away."

Father: "Yes, and he gave away the Church of England. It is a proof that Protestants are united only when warring against the Catholic Church. But he gives himself away still more in saying, on page 30: 'The Methodist Episcopate has now been before the world for more than a century.' The Methodist Episcopacy is to the Catholic Episcopacy what 1 is to 19. What a ratio?"

Knox: "Drop the Episcopacy. As I stated before, I do not believe in it."

Bro. Wesley: "Rev. McGrew is a Methodist Episcopalian, because 'the Faith of the Church is founded upon the Word of God, which is contained in the Holy Scriptures. It is embodied in the Apostles' creed and the Twenty-five Articles. In these every applicant for membership is required to confess his belief. The Articles are an abridgment of the Thirty-nine Articles of the Church of England. Fifteen have been entirely omitted. These omissions were made for the sake of securing greater simplicity, catholicity and consistency in doctrine. Without quoting the language of the Articles, a few general statements will serve to show why some of them were omitted. The teaching of the Methodist Episcopal Church is consistently Arminian without being Pelagian. She holds that salvation is possible for every man; that all persons dying in infancy are saved; that those who have not heard the Gospel are not necessarily lost. Mr. Wesley wrote concerning Marcus Aurelius: "I doubt not this is one o f the 'many' who shall 'come from the East and the West and sit down with Abraham, Isaac and Jacob,' while the children of the 'Kingdom,' nominal Christians, are shut out.'" He also spoke confidently of the salvation of Roman Catholics. Those Articles which were retained are thoroughly liberal and Catholic. As to the Sacraments, the Methodist Episcopal Church symbolizes with the Church of England. She teaches a real, although a spiritual, presence in the Holy Communion. Baptism is a sign of regeneration; but one may be baptized without being regenerated, and regenerated without first having been baptized. In accordance with the. command under the Old Covenant, children are admitted into the church by Baptism. The mode is not essential to the validity of the Sacrament. Hence Methodist Episcopalians baptize either by sprinkling, pouring or immersion. The church does not teach that baptism is not a saving ordinance, and at the same time exclude from the Table of the Lord all who have not been immersed. "

Pastor: "Our faith, too, is founded on the Word of God. All denominations claim this, consequently it is no argument in favor of the M. E. Church."

Archdeacon: "*Fifteen* (Articles) *have been entirely omitted.* Unless the Brother can convince us that the omitted ones were not taught by God, it seems to me there would be a good reason for not adhering to the said church."

Exhorter:. "He says your Articles are *inconsistent;* if so, there is a good reason for omitting them. Evidently, God did not teach inconsistent doctrines."

Archdeacon: "But this is a mere assertion, the proof has not been furnished. Furthermore, *Catholic* means *general.* I do not understand how *omissions* can promote Catholicity. We must believe all God has been pleased to reveal. In short, Mr. McGrew gives no reason whatever why his church should have the preference to mine or any other."

Father: "You and I agree on this point, Archdeacon. This writer also believes in infant baptism. Yet he makes the statement that one may be baptised *without being regenerated*. It surely would be refreshing to have his explanation on this question in the case of an infant."

Exhorter: "I have come to the conclusion that the Protestant churches have been badly represented in *Why I am What I am*."

Father: "When we take into consideration the disadvantages under which these men labor, I think they have performed their task well. It does not become falsehood to wear the veil of truth. Its horns will show themselves, for truth will prevail in spite of everything. As to the fifteen articles, Bro. Wesley, we need not go into details. Read our books and you will be convinced that Christ has taught many doctrines which you do not teach. In the SHORT LINE it is fully demonstrated that the Bible is not and cannot be the *Rule of Faith*. Therefore, Article V. must fall to the ground. Article XVIII. treats on the Lord's supper; it, too, as we have seen, when the Archdeacon had the floor, falls of its own weight. The church is called by St. Paul the *pillar of truth*, Let it eliminate one revealed truth, or teach a single false doctrine, and it is no longer a *pillar of truth*, but a tower of Babel."

Bro. Wesley: "My name sake was a good man. This, at least, is an indisputable fact."

Father: "I know nothing against the moral character of the man. But a good man may have been a bad boy. Read his father's letter, dated at Wroote, Jan. 26, 1725. It is given in full by Tyerman, vol. I.,

p 30. Furthermore he was an ordained minister of
one church (Ch. of Engl.) and he established another
quite different from the one established by Christ.
No good man, unless gross ignorance excuses him, will
do this."

Bro. Wesley: "Be this as it may, the missionary
work of the M. E. Church has done a great deal of
good in this world."

Father: "Mention, if you can, a single heathen
nation converted to Christianity by their missionaries."

Exhorter: "What have the Catholics done in this
direction?"

Father: "St. Patrick converted heathen Ireland."

Bro. Wesley: "Give us credit for the great temperance movement, coming like an avalanche over this
glorious country."

Father: "By temperance you mean total abstinence; for the former means according to Webster,
moderate indulgence of the appetites. I admit you have
kept many a one from filling a drunkard's grave. But
the end does not justify the means which you use and
which I detest."

Bro. Wesley: "How so, Father?"

Father: "You misrepresent the truth—you tell the
people, it is wrong to *touch, handle, smell or taste intoxi-
cants.* This is not true, testified by our Savior at the
marriage feast and Last Supper. Tell the truth and
then go on with the good work. We are helping you.
Look at our numerous total abstinence organizations
throughout the length and breadth of the land.

On the other hand, let me ask you to help us a little
in stopping one of the greatest evils of the age. I
mean divorce followed by marriage. In this your

church is very lax. I have known a Methodist preacher married to a divorced woman, a preacher at the head of a respectable congregation."

Bro. Wesley: "It may have been a case in which divorce is granted by divine dispensation: 'Whosoever put away his wife, except it be for fornication, and shall marry another, committeth adultery.'" (Matt. 19, 9.)

Father: "It is admitted by all critics, that, frequently, one text must be explained by another. Let us do so in the case before us. In St. Mark we read: 'Whosoever shall put away his wife, and marry another, committeth adultery against her. And if the wife shall put away her husband, and be married to another, she committeth adultery.' (10, 11. 12.) St. Paul confirms this: 'To them that are married, not I, but the Lord commandeth, that the wife depart not from her husband; and if she depart, that she remain *unmarried*, or be reconciled to her husband. And let not the husband put away his wife.' (I Cor., 7, 10. 11.) What follows? A man may put away an adulterous wife, but during her life he must remain single."

Bro. Wesley: "I cannot see why a man should be punished on account of the unfaithfulness of his wife."

Father: "Your doctrine leads to immorality—yes, polygamy. You might as well say, why should the one be punished when the other is a confirmed invalid? Divorce, even on account of unfaithfulness, does not sanction a second marriage. During the first 1500 years it was almost unheard-of. Divorce, heartbroken wives, unprotected children, are the fruits of the Reformation. Instead of warring continually against a glass of wine, which a man may take without transgressing the laws of God, we beg you to assist us to fight Mormonism, both in and out of Utah. I am proud to say no Catholic Priest stoops so low as to solemnize such a marriage for the sake of a $5.00 or $10.00 fee."

Exhorter: "Father, we have spent a very pleasant evening, but the time has come when we must go."

Father: "Thank you, gentlemen. Permit me, however, to give you the following POINTERS: Never say:

1. That the Church of Christ, established almost 1900 years ago, was a failure; for you put the lie in the mouth of our blessed Lord, saying, 'Thou art Peter, and upon this rock I will build my church; and the gates of hell shall not prevail against it.' (Matt. 16-18).

2. That your churches can be traced back to Christ and His Twelve Apostles. History testifies to the contrary. The oldest Protestant Church is the Lutheran, which to-day is not 400 years old. Compared to the Catholic Church, it is still wearing its swaddling clothes—and has fundamentally changed since Luther.

3. That the Reformers were good men. Historians deny it, and the Reformers prove it by calling each other hard names with vouchers for their truthfulness.

4. That the Bible is the *Rule of Faith*. Christ never commanded his chosen Twelve to go and *write*, but to go and *teach*. Your doctrine is a powerful weapon in the hands of a fellow like Ingersoll, whose followers are never Catholics.

5. That you Protestants agree among yourselves on essentials. You disagree even on Baptism, not only as to its mode, but also as to its necessity. Your churches are like so many cockle-shells tossed to and fro by *every wind of doctrine*."

SIDE SWITCHES.

BOOKLET SECOND.—TRUE SIDE-SWITCHES.

A WORD TO EXPECTANT READERS.

Although we enjoy the patness of smart retorts as well as any one, when the subject matter will bear such everyday usage, you, dear and intelligent inquirer, will feel with us that there are things too high above the tone of common conversation to admit of a similar license.

This Booklet, therefore, even if it retain the popular title fitted to our general line of argumentative dialogue, dealing as it does with the most Sacred Rites and Ceremonies of the Church, must of necessity be sparing of tempting expressions, and rise in dignity of language with its holy and awful subjects.

BOOKLET II.—TRUE SIDE-SWITCHES.

1. OUTSIDE THE CHURCH.

SCENE—VILLA SAINT LAWRENCE

CHARACTERS:

Thomas Objector,	*Uncommercial Traveler.*
O. T. Bee,	*Professor.*
Lady Wilde Ruskin,	*Father.*

Thomas Objector: "Father, you have interested me so much by your answers in former friendly talks on Religion and the Roman Catholic Church, that naturally, I have spoken of your courtesy and directness.

"I have brought with me a few of my friends who will introduce themselves by their queries from their different standpoints, and talk less familiarly than we did. By shunting the Five Denominations represented by their ministers, as badly damaged empty cars, laid up indefinitely for repairs on side-tracks, you have stirred up opposition and objection to your own SIDE-SWITCHES. Now, what do you mean by the hard lines you have put us upon?"

Father: "Well, Thomas, I have had to rout you on the Main Line, and now I propose, for your own good, principally, to prove to you that the accessories of the True Church are the True SIDE-SWITCHES OF THE SHORT LINE. We shall use almost exclusively official books and manuals.."

Uncom. Traveler: "Rev. Father, I have gone many thousand miles in my time, and become curious about you Catholics, your manifold ceremonies and peculiar ways of action, which people sometimes irreverently calls 'mummeries.'"

Father: "Exactly. Wishing to drop the R. R. metaphor, and come down to business, I will say that these ceremonies and 'mummeries' are the outward clothing and expressions of doctrines. They are thought lightly of, and more or less ridiculed, because the outside world don't understand them. I'll explain them."

Lady Wilde Ruskin: "Do, Rev. Father, please. I am of the High Church, or a Ritualist, as they are pleased to name us, and we have many things in common with you in our introduction of religious pomp."

Father: "Yes, my lady, pomp, I fear, without the truth to sustain it—clothes of the finest upon a dumb statue. But to keep order, let Thomas have the lead."

Thomas: "Thank you. I shall object first, that priests and nuns wear such old-fashioned black suits—cassocks and habits, I believe you call them."

Father: "You will understand that the Church is necessarily an old institution, dating back through all these centuries to Roman, Grecian, and even Jewish times. Have you never read how the Almighty God prescribed the very garments of the priests and levites of the old law? Consult Chap. XXVIII. and XXIX. Exodus."

Thomas: "Excuse me, I have read, too, that all these things, together with sacrifices and minute ceremonies of the Law of Moses, were abolished by Christ."

Father: "Abolished? Take care what strong words
you use. Christ came not to destroy, but to replace—
to fulfill the types of the old law. It is nowhere stated
that the *use* of certain distinctive dress and the essential ceremonies of religious worship were forbidden
or even discouraged. Now to your query. The everyday dress of priests at home and of religious are fash-
ioned, if you wish to use the word, on common sense
combined with costumes prevailing at different per-
iods among original races. Many habits are but
modified from the common dress of the times. The
cassock is black, as well as the habits of various nuns,
because of their being worn by persons who do not
follow varying and worldly modes, and are meant as
a becoming apparel for sober-minded men and women
who cast off finery and devote themselves to eternity.
The priest's garment resembles the manly toga of the
Romans. The Pope's white wool cassock denotes his
singular and conspicuous position as the Vicar of
Christ, the good shepherd."

O. T. Bee: "But what is the use of Bishops ap-
pearing in such gorgeous colors? I am a Catholic
myself, but I do object, as a republican, to such princely attire—even if the Jewish priests dressed so finely."

Father: "Ah! Do you? Remember that the
Bishop's official garb at home is very modest—a dull
purple, with slight red trimmings, or even a black cassock with purple buttons. We shall get upon the
subject of 'princely attire' presently."

Thomas: "Leaving that aside, as I enter a Catholic Church I find men, women and children dipping
their hands in the water stoops at the doors and making some signs with the water. What is this for?"

Father: "This is Holy Water, with which they sign themselves with the sign of the cross—1st, to remind them to put worldly thoughts out of their head; 2d, to ask and obtain the blessing of God for their worship and worthy reception of the sacraments; 3d, in two words, to denote their allegiance to Christ—and keep the devil off."

Lady Wilde Ruskin: "Why, Father, you shock us. *Keep the devil off?*"

Father: "Yes, Madame, nothing less. The blessing of the salt to put into the water reads: 'Wherever thou art sprinkled let every delusion and wickedness of the devil, and all unclean spirits fly and depart when adjured by Him who shall come to judge the living and the dead and the world by fire.' And listen to this exorcism—or driving out of the devil from the water used: 'That thou mayst have strength to uproot and cast out the enemy himself, and his apostate angels.' It is calculated also to 'drive away disease,' or the 'blast of pestilence' and 'deliver from hurt,' 'healing by the invocation of the 'holy name,' through the holy angel from Heaven who is bidden to 'guard, cherish, protect, visit and defend all those assembled in the house of God.' Similar are blessings of palms, ashes, candles."

O. T. Bee: "And so *that* is the reason the priest sprinkles the congregation with Holy Water—and uses it in all sorts of blessings of persons and objects?"

Father: "Yes, Mr. Bee, didn't you know that?"

O. T. Bee: "Well, I ought to, I acknowledge."

Father: "As water is an effective symbol, both temporal and spiritual, especially, as all know, in the Sacrament of Baptism, permit me to add that this first and most important Sacrament, by the sacred rubrics of its administration, commences right in this porch of the church. The candidate, called cate- chumen--because he is catechised and taught the rudiments of faith and divine law—if an adult, before his *spiritual* admission, is also obliged to confess his unworthiness by knocking at the *material* church door to beg admittance. He is asked:

"What dost thou ask of the Church of God?"

Answer—"Faith."

"What doth faith lead thee to?"

Answer—"To life everlasting."

Presently the priest, clad in violet or penitential stole, stoops suddenly and breathes three times on the child's or adult's face—imitating God's action in creating life in Adam—and gives his first command to Satan: "Depart from him, thou unclean spirit, and give place to the Holy Ghost the Paraclete"—placing the holy sign of the cross on the forehead and breast of the candidate. So you see, already, my friends, why Catholics use Holy Water with the sign of salvation on entering a church. Even here again we have the blessing of salt, symbol of wisdom and wholeness from corruption, followed by the first formal exorcism with the triple sign, in the name of the Three Divine Persons."

Thomas: "I hear, by the way, there are some very vigorous curses pronounced by the exorcists and priests at Baptism."

Father: "No doubt, and for the best of reasons. The doctrine underlying this strong language is the horrid conviction that the minister meets the 'Ruined Archangel' face to face, tho' invisibly by other than the eyes of faith, and he does not mince words. 'Unclean spirit' is mild beside, 'accursed outcast,' or more literally, 'accursed and damned wretch;' and twice thereafter he is called 'accursed devil.' Then after laying on of a hand the priest leads the person in by extending to him the extremity of the stole. And, by the way, would not my kind objectors be please i to enter our church over the way? There I can illustrate better by pointing to objects. It just happens that the Blessed Sacrament is not in the tabernacle and we can converse in a low tone."

All: "By all means, Father, at your service."

Exeunt Omnes.

II.   HOW IT LOOKS INSIDE.

Uncom. Traveler: (In half whisper) "Umph! This feels solemn! Father, what *is* the secret you priests possess of getting up such interiors of churches as to impress the beholder and rivet his attention, even before the sermon?"

Father: "It may seem a secret, or even magic to some. To Catholics it is the most natural of all things to make the house of God as unlike all other houses, not even excepting palaces, as possible. We build and ornament for God, giving him the most precious products of nature and all the fine arts— Poetry, Architecture, Music, Painting, Sculpture, and magnificent Ritual, which is, in very deed, a LIVING COMBINATION of THEM all. It is, however, also for men's sake—to impress truth by lively and moving images, whether addressed to the eye, ear, sense of delicate perfume, or susceptibility to outward, beautiful and instructive forms. In one word, to move the mind and soul through the natural medium of the senses."

Lady Wilde Ruskin: "I agree with you, Father. We ought to have everything attractive in church. The first Reformers made a great mistake in baring the walls of churches, tearing down superb pictures, demolishing fine statuary, and doing away generally with all the aesthetic in religion—making the Gothic Cathedrals and Renaissance Temples mere white-washed meeting houses."

Thomas: "Have a care, my lady, you do not tread on some one's corns."

Lady Wilde: "To see how almost all the denominations, except, perhaps, the Quakers, are giving up their effete notions and following the fashion of imitating us of the true grand branches—Roman, Anglican and Grecian—it would seem that persons have dispensed with their tenderness of foot in this regard."

Father: No quarrelling among yourselves, especially in the church, the one which has taught you all —all the truth you possess, and given you patterns how to express it in your churches and in such ceremonies as you observe. Only be careful you do not stick in the ceremonies and leave the doctrine expressed by them in the background. This is pictorial hypocrisy. But let us return to our immediate subject. You notice the cruciform shape of the church. In St. Peter's at Rome, and indeed in many other grand churches, the altar is placed just at the bi-section of the cross, the priest in that case invariably remaining with his face turned *towards* the people. This reminds one vividly of our Lord upon the cross, which is in truth not only typified by the Mass but is actually, though mystically carried out."

Lady Wilde: "I love to see the sign of the cross glorified and used upon the person. You know, Father we use it actually in baptism."

Father: "Yes, but I wish your church had the courage of its convictions and would not leave the making of the holy sign actually optional with parents or others, as your Ritual Book of Common Prayer allows."

Thomas: "Protestant churches, even in cities, have no place to kneel in prayer, usually, or the kneeling benches are not used."

Father: "I am glad you advert to comparatively so slight a matter. It makes, however, a decided contrast between the filial conduct of the church and the cool step-son kind of piety encouraged, if not taught, outside of its communion. Many of you separated brethren only bow the head. I have been present at the opening of Congress at Washington and remarked that during the chaplain's oratorial effort, meant for a prayer, but few of the senators and *none of the boy pages* even bowed the head. Our service, on the contrary, requires sure-enough kneeling, on both knees, for a length of time too; the bowing of the head, either standing, kneeling or sitting, at mention, for example, of the august name of JESUS CHRIST. Rubrics sometimes demand the prostration of the body full length before the altar of the Lord. On Good Friday and at Ordinations, the priest or candidates lies flat on his face for some moments, to show, in the one case, the completeness of the sacrifice of

Christ, and in the other, the total surrender of body
and soul henceforward to the service of the Creator.
Now, are not these positions befitting for sinful
creatures before their Lord, God, Judge and Creator?"

Thomas: "Oh! but remember we Protestants
worship 'in spirit and truth,' and do not think it
necessary to display piety by unbecoming postures."

Father: "All I can answer is that as long as we
live in our bodies here upon earth we are bound to
pay homage to God by acting as human, mortal
beings, and can not ordinarily separate worship of
soul from worship of body without running risk of
not worshiping at all. To be sure, we humble the
mind, and these outward prostrations are only signs
and expressions of spirit worship."

Uncom. Traveler: "Still, it occurs to me, Rev.
Father, you mistake the force of the objection. You
will acknowledge that the main point is *to worship in
soul*; which, as your philosophers tell us, is the
form of the body; and if we can and do get along
without these outside helps, by means of representa-
tions to the senses, the worship of the body or outward manifestations are unnecessary. Hermits need
no pictures or symbols."

Father: "You unconsciously furnish an answer
to your own objection. How many are hermits or
so spiritual that they need no sensible helps to excite
devotion? To settle the matter and put the whole
response in a nutshell—God Himself in the Old Law
and Christ in the New laid down and enjoined the
use of sensible things for the general run of mankind. Christ, our Lord, as we have intimated and
will explain more fully as we proceed, attaches grace

to symbolic Rites, and uses in every Sacrament some one or other outward sign or sensible, tangible object as the indication and medium of spiritual grace. Water and words in Baptism; oil and forms of sentences for Confirmation, Orders, Extreme   Unction. So we are obliged to worship outwardly and inwardly. But, let us postpone these questions to better time and place."

O. T. Bee: "That's what I say. Explain these pictures, images on the altars and all the rest, for I could never defend their use very well against unbelievers."

Father: "Nor, 'give a reason for the faith that is in you,' because you were not practical enough a Catholic to post yourself by reading or hearing instructions."

Lady Wilde: "High Church member as I am, I never could put these statues and pictures to such uses as Catholics make of them. I believe in making religion attractive and beautiful, but we draw the line at praying before these altars or figures. It is against the second commandment."

Father: "You surely mean the last part of the *first* commandment.   But you rebels from the Church have had the assurance to re-divide the commandments, in order to get in your fling at the Church on the score of idolatry. Now, the end of the first commandment forbids the making of such images as are intended for actual worship; for it adds after the enumeration, 'Thou shalt not adore nor serve them.' And, here, Professor, I shall have to call in your learning in the ancient languages to help me out. You know what word is employed in the ancient

Septuaginst Greek version of the Old Testament, used by the Apostles and early Church, for what is ordinarily translated as 'images?' "

Professor: "Yes, sir, I happen to recall the exact word—it is *eidolon*—from which our English word is directly derived. In fact reduced to its root it is the same—*idol*."

Father: "And is not the first and proper signification of that Greek word 'idols?' "

Professor: "It is; and the context bears it out."

Father: "Therefore, the prohibition is against idols, or images for idolatrous worship. For it is trite to say, that the Lord God of Israel commanded statues of angels to be stationed on the Ark, and made Moses display a brazen serpent, and Solomon paint angels and erect brass oxen.

"As we touch the resemblance of the Church to the Tabernacle and Temple of the Jews, let us observe, that the porch of a Christian Church, especially as in early times devoted to Catechumens and penitents, corresponds to the Jewish outer court of the Gentiles and proselytes. The court of the Jewish women, separated off to themselves, was copied strictly in the catacombs and early church and is yet imitated in Catholic countries—the men retaining the 'place of the faithful' in the body of the Church.

"The old Holy of Holies was curtained off by a heavy portiere of costly material, just about where our communion rail now stands; which latter fully represents the magnificent rood-screens of European Cathedrals, and the ancient hangings actually drawn across the sanctuary and excluding the gaze of the faithful during the Canon of the Mass. Inside of the railing or curtain, the Law of Moses placed the Altar of Incense towards the middle, with the Seven-branch Candlestick on one side and the Table of Show-bread on the other—prefiguring our lamp and the seven large candlesticks used when a Bishop pontificates, the incense used in High Mass, and the blessed bread yet distributed at the offertory in some churches. Inside the Ark of the Covenant three things were allowed—the budded rod of Aaron, the Tables of the Law and the Pot of incorruptible manna, the 'Bread from Heaven'—plainly fore-shadowing the authority of the Christian priesthood to teach the law and dispense the Bread of Life.

"As we shall go out now, while awaiting the arrival of the Rt. Rev. Bishop for Confirmation at the Solemn High Mass, we may take a general view of the pictures and statues on the walls, observing that the Sanctuary or Holy of Holies, is cut off, and raised above the main body of the Church, by the communion rail. There, at the right, you have the altar of the Blessed Virgin and the Baptistery or Baptismal Font. On the left the Altar of St. Joseph, the statue of our Lord with Patron Saint, Saint Lawrence, and beyond them the Confessional. The main altar, with its candlesticks, crucifix, missal, tabernacle, side-table or credence; on the platform the bells or gongs. Swinging in mid-air, facing the tabernacle in the middle of the altar, is the silver lamp, in which a taper is kept burning when the Blessed Sacrament is present.

Now, we may go out into the fresh summer air, and making ourselves comfortable under the boughs of a spreading oak discuss these matters at our ease."

III. PREPARING FOR THE PRESENCE.

Father: "My friend, I feel we are warming towards each other, differ as we may, because we are all conscientious in our belief and honest in our convictions. So I can respect your faith in your religion, tho' I must combat what I know to be your errors. And in your turn you think none the less of me on account of my truth-barbed retorts. Now, I wish to ask what is your general impression of the interior of a Catholic Church?"

Uncom. Traveler: "I must say it reminds me, if you will not take offense at the comparison, of a kind of religious theatre, where there may be a serious drama, or even mild tragedy represented, but never a comedy."

Lady Wilde: "I am just in ecstacies over it— barring, of course, what I beg leave to consider the extravagance of the devotion of Catholics to others than our Lord, and well, perhaps, I might add the Virgin Mary."

O. T. Bee: "I, as a believing Catholic, tho' somewhat liberal in my views, can not but admire the grand Ritual of the Church and think the stage is worthy of its acting. I am candid tho' in adding that it brings the priests and bishops too much into prominence. I would like more democracy, and less penance and hell-fire for the laity."

Father: "Permit me to interrupt a moment to state, that Mr. Bee does not represent the true feeling of Catholics who are practical and, I would say, better instructed. Moreover, I believe we may dis-

pense with the Professor's and Mr. Objector's opinion for the nonce. I will draw them out as I proceed, and they may have a tilt at me when they
please. I will not reject the comparison of the
Traveler, for, indeed, there is much truth in the idea
that the Church sets out purposely to enact the
mysteries of religion and place them as vividly as
possibly before the senses—Thomas, you seem to
object."

Thomas: "You are mistaken this time. My look
only meant that I wanted to ask what all this fine interior and the superb acting of the Ritual point to?
What is the central idea?"

Father: "You have divined my thought exactly.
I do not wish to enter into controversy about the Real
Presence, or the Ceremonies of Mass and our public
worship; I will let the church speak her faith *by her
gestures*. But I am desirous to state plainly the doctrine whence all this pomp has its source. It is that
the Catholic Church considers her house of worship
the earthly palace of the Almighty Eternal. Not in a
general way, but as an actual habitation of a really
present God. He is enthroned truly and substantially, though invisibly to our eyes, in the tabernacle,
and at the consecration of the Mass on the altar stone
itself. Now, all the reverence shown about the altar
is directed towards that Awful Presence, mighty in its
dreadful reality, soothing and blessing in the humility and love displayed in the mode and form of its
manifestation to faith. You surely cannot accuse us
of intentional or formal idolatry if you admit that
we *believe* Christ our Blessed Savior to be present in
person. The belief to the contrary, to-wit: That

Christ is *not* substantially and personally present in
the churches of the sects, is the plain reason why they
discard all manifestations of devotion towards a PRES-
ENT GOD."

Chorus of Objectors: "How dare you impugn our
faith in God's presence, literally everywhere?" .

Father: "God's presence everywhere? But we are
speaking of the Catholic dogma which holds that
CHRIST ALMIGHTY, in His whole sacred person, *as
God and as man*—His body, blood, soul and divinity,
is offered on our altar and is actually present in the
tabernacle as the adorable Host. You, of course,
cannot hold that Christ, body and blood and soul are
really present everywhere—that is absolutely against
faith and reason. As to the proofs for the Presence
that makes a Roman Catholic Church but a minor
heaven—the very vestibule of Paradise, I must leave
them to controversialists proper. One remark will
suffice here. How comes it that Protestants exalt faith
at the expense of everything else—church, priesthood,
works of penance, and still cannot bring themselves
to believe the principal tenet of Christianity; *that
Christ abides with us forever!*"

Thomas: "We believe He does abide with us in
spirit!"

Father: "Our Lord could not be said to abide with
the church forever if He were not present with His
children, as God made man. This means that when
He disappeared from mortal eyes, He must have left
the substance of His human nature in some other
form accessible to the faithful. THE GOD-MAN ABIDES
IN THE EUCHARIST. You show, in one word, a most
lamentable lack of faith and confidence in His repeated

and clear pledges in Scripture, that His utmost act of love is His true giving of Himself for the Food of souls in the chief Sacrament."

Professor: "That is a new and beautiful view of the case."

Thomas: "There is the church bell ringing. Had we not better return thither?"

Father: "Yes, and we shall be in time to listen to the Pastor instructing the adults for Baptism and preparing the candidates for Confirmation. On the way, I will explain that the two great times for the solemn administration of these Sacraments are precisely about the feasts of Resurrection and of the Descent of the Holy Ghost. Amid the poetical and sublime ceremonies of Holy Week and Pentecost-tide, the fonts are blessed and water consecrated—the priests and deacons meanwhile preparing converts for re-birth in Baptism and perfect faith in Confirmation."

Professor: "Ah! by good fortune, the Pastor is just leading in the converts by that picturesque ceremony of the extension of the stole. Oh! how I enjoy this."

Father: "Very good, Professor. I see the priest has finished the first instruction and is proceeding with the ceremonies of Baptism. We shall quietly look on as you translate the Latin for us."

IV. CEREMONIES OF THE RE-BIRTH.

Professor: "First comes the loud recitation of the Creed, and then the Lord's Prayer. On the way the minister pronounces the last formal exorcism.

I translate: I exorcise thee, every unclean spirit, in the name of God, the Father † Almighty, in the name of Jesus Christ, His Son † our Lord and Judge, and in the power of the Holy † Ghost, that thou depart from *this creature* of God, N., which our Lord hath pleased to call unto His holy temple, that *it* may be made the temple of the living God, and that the Holy Ghost may dwell therein * * * Notice the neuter 'it.' (*Then wetting his thumb with spittle, as our Lord did in the cure of the deaf and dumb, he touches the ears and nostrils, saying:*) 'Ephpheta, that is to say, Be opened, for a. savor of of sweetness.' "

(*Follows the renouncing of the Devil, Sin and its occasion.*)

'Priest: N.   Dost thou renounce Satan?'

'Sponsor: I do renounce him.'

'Priest: And all his works?"

'Spon.:   I do renounce them.'

'P.:   And all his pomps.'

'Spon.:   I do renounce them.'

(*Anointing the breast and between the shoulders in the form of a cross*).

'I anoint thee † with the oil of salvation in Christ Jesus, our Lord, that thou mayest have eternal life.'

(*Here changing the violet stole of penance for the white one of joy and innocence he receives the short profession of faith*).

'N.   Dost thou believe in God the Father, Creator? Dost thou believe in Jesus Christ, His only Son? Dost thou believe in the Holy Ghost, the Holy Catholic Church, the communion of saints, the forgiveness of sins, the resurrection of the body and life everlasting?' Finally, asking the consent of the person: 'Wilt thou be baptized.'

(*Receiving affirmative answers, the minister pours the water thrice on the head in form of a cross, saying once only and distinctly*).

'N., I BAPTIZE THEE IN THE NAME OF THE FATHER † AND OF THE SON † AND OF THE HOLY † GHOST.'

Father: "I beg you to note that another human

being has thus become a child of God by being grafted as a member on the mystical body of Christ, whose blood of redemption has just been applied to the soul by means of "water and the Holy Ghost"— the form of life. For, the Sacraments effect in the soul what the outward signs or ceremonies denote as applied to the body. Read on, Professor."

Professor: "Anointing with chrism the crown of the head the minister pursues: 'May Almighty God, the Father of our Lord Jesus Christ, He who hath regenerated thee by water and the Holy Ghost, and given thee remission of all thy sins, anoint † thee with the chrism of salvation, in the same Christ Jesus Our Lord, unto life everlasting. Amen.

Peace be with thee!"

(Spreading a white linen cloth, in token of the white garments worn for some days in ancient times by the newly baptized, on the head:)

'Receive this white garment, which mayst thou bear without spot before the judgment seat of our Lord Jesus Christ, that thou mayst have life everlasting.' Finally, giving a lighted candle: 'Receive this burning light, and keep thy Baptism so as to be without blame. Observe the commandments of God, that when the Lord shall come to the nuptials, thou mayst meet Him together with all the saints in the heavenly court, and mayest have eternal life, and live forever and ever, amen!'

V. RITES OF CONFIRMATION.

Scene—Balcony, Overlooking the Sanctuary.

Father: "Now that we have listened to the lucid explanation of the pastor on Confirmation, we understand that this sacrament is really a completion of baptism. We that are reborn have been adopted by God the Father as His true children, brethren of His only Divine Son and rightful heirs of His Son. But, as great Will has it, an infant is a weak, puling creature, 'mewling and puking in the nurse's arms,' and must bide its time to grow into the possession of its powers of body and the ripening of the faculties of the mind. So the infant, or just regenerated soul, must be nursed by the imbibing of the Holy Spirit's gifts and be matured by His fruits into a perfect Christian and well-armed soldier of Christ.

"Though little children are confirmed according to a custom in parts of the world, for instance in South America, the ordinary discipline of the church requires the age of seven and generally ten or twelve, just before puberty, and fuller instruction in the rudiments of faith and law, in the candidates for confirmation. The incipient man or woman is then fed on the Bread of Life."

Professor: "We find from the Ritual for Confirmation that chrism is used. Now, what is Chrism, and what is its meaning?"

Father: "The official manual explains: Chrism is an ointment composed of olive or sweet oil and balsam. The outward anointing means the inward consecration by the Holy Ghost. Oil is used to strengthen; is smooth and mild—representing the diffusion of grace and the infusion of virtue. Balsam, employed for wounds and to prevent corruption, is an apt image of preservation."

Thomas: "The Bishop approaches clad in his pontifical vestments."

Father: "The Bishop, as a High Priest and

Shepherd, is clothed in head-dress, called a mitre, in the Cope, a linen alb, confined by a cincture, and the stole; carrying a crozier or shepherd's crook in his left hand and wearing a ring on the right, with which hand he anoints.

"The vestments are copied after the requirements of Pontiffs in the old Law. Aaron wore a mitre or priestly crown of low form, was clad in femoral or inside close fitting linen robe, over which was worn the outside linen bound by a girdle between the navel and the breast. Over all at last the ephod or cope with clasp of two onyxes, and, strapped on his breast, the plate of gold bearing twelve precious stones representing the twelve tribes of Israel, whose names they bore.

"You notice the attire—princely as it is, Mr. O. T. Bee—of the Bishop is very similar in its particulars in almost every instance. Lo! Confirmation begins. Professor please translate as he proceeds."

Professor: "(*He prays with joined hands*). May the Holy Ghost descend upon you, and may the power of the Most High preserve you from sins.'
(*Signing himself, he recites the verses*):
' † Our help is in the name of the Lord.'
Ans. 'Who hath made heaven and earth.'
'O Lord, hear my prayer.'
Ans. 'And let my cry come unto Thee.'
'The Lord be with you.'
Ans. 'And with thy spirit.'
(*Extending his hands over those to be confirmed*).
'Let us pray: Almighty and eternal God, who hast vouchsafed to regenerate these thy servants by water and the Holy Ghost, and hast given them forgiveness of all their sins, send forth Thy seven-fold Spirit, the Holy Comforter.'
Ans. 'Amen.'

'The Spirit of Wisdom and Understanding.'
Ans. 'Amen.'
'The Spirit of Counsel and Fortitude.'
Ans. 'Amen.'
'The Spirit of Knowledge and Piety.'
Ans. 'Amen.'
"Fill them with the spirit of Thy fear, and sign them with the sign of the cross † of Christ, in Thy mercy, unto life eternal!
Ans. 'Amen.'
(*Signing them with Holy Chrism on the forehead*).
'N., I SIGN THEE WITH THE SIGN OF THE CROSS † AND I CONFIRM THEE WITH THE CHRISM OF SALVATION.'
(*Blessing them three times he ends*):
'In the name of the Father † and of the Son and of the Holy † Ghost.'
Ans. 'Amen.'
(*Stroking each one on the cheek*) 'Peace be with thee.'
After the antiphon: 'Confirm, O God, what Thou hast wrought in us, from Thy Holy Temple which is in Jerusalem,' laying aside the mitre and turning toward the altar, the Bishop prays: 'O Lord, show thy mercy upon us.'
'Ans: And grant us Thy salvation.'
'O Lord, hear my prayer.'
Ans: And let my cry come unto Thee.'

LET US PRAY.

'O God, who didst give to Thine Apostles the Holy Ghost and didst ordain through them and their successors He should be given to the rest of the faithful; look mercifully upon our unworthy service; and grant that the hearts of those whose foreheads we have anointed with holy chrism, and signed with the sign. of the holy cross, may, by the same Holy Ghost coming down upon them and graciously abiding within them, be made the temple of His glory.'
The Blessing: 'May the Lord † bless you out of Sion, that you may see the good things of Jerusalem all the days of your life, and may have life everlasting '
Ans: 'Amen!'"

VI. PHYSICIAN IN CASE OF SERIOUS ACCI-
DENT.

Father: "My friend, whilst the ministers are preparing for the High Mass and the pastor is hearing
the last confessions we may recur to the rites of
Penance or Confession. And first, though our hick-
ory Catholic, Mr. O. T. Bee, hasn't been to Confession for a long time, I can rely upon him to report
what is done in Confession when one goes. Can't I?"

O. T. Bee: "Your remark is not very flattering
one way, but then I'm not ignorant exactly and may
answer: I learned when a child that it's all humbug
about a Catholic getting off so easy as Protestants
imagine. *They* have the easy way of slipping out I
imagine, and I often wish I could adopt it. Why,
gentlemen and my lady, you have to be drilled in
catechism from the time you can toddle, and then
generally go to confession, after you are old enough
to commit mortal sin, (about seven years), every
three months. The old Church, after all, under-
stands nature pretty well, and knocks the bottom out
of the fine supposition that little children can do no
harm much, and go straight to heaven without ado,
in case they die before the age of twelve or fourteen."

Uncom. Traveler: "Spare us preaching, Mr. Bee,
please. But tell us how you go to Confession and
drop your bundle of sins at the priest's feet, and still
run out scot free and as clean all over as a perch fresh
from the water."

O. T. Bee: "You all take the cue from Father
here to pounce on me. But I'll let you know I'll
stand more from him than from you."

Father: "Peace now in the camp. Why, they will hear you quarreling in the Church! Go on, Mr. Bee."

O. T. Bee: "I once heard a priest praise an answer given by a country lad to the question: 'What do you do after you have prayed for the grace of a good Confession?' '*Why, I hunt up my sins,*' said he. You hunt 'em up, generally, by thinking over your duties at home, Church and school or society in which you have been. You may refer to the 'tables of sin' in your prayer-book, asking questions on the faults against the commands of God and the Church and state of life. And you must be particular to search out even the number of times you have committed mortal sin—as each one of them is bound to come out. Then you endeavor to excite contrition or hearty and perfect sorrow, if you can, purely for the love of God. This, I believe, is so satisfactory that by it mortal sins may be forgiven, in a case of necessity, even without confession. Is it no so, Father?"

Father: "Yes, provided you desire to confess, if you had an opportunity. Besides, you must be prepared to forgive injuries and repair scandals and injustice towards others. For example, if you have stolen goods of any amount, you must see the same or their equivalent restored—even if it be a case of defrauding the Government. This is where 'conscience' money comes in."

Uncom. Traveler: "Pretty good institution that makes a sleek thief disgorge his ill-gotten gains! I've known cases of thousands of dollars being refunded to Government officials through the confessional."

Father: "Father Tom Burke once referred in public to $150,000 he had received from a penitent for restitution."

O. T. Bee: "You may then get even your venial sins together, if you really repent of them—though it is not strictly required, since you may obtain pardon of them in various ways, out of confession. But the Church makes a marked distinction between grievous and lesser sins, contrary to Protestants, who think all alike."

Thomas: "If we had time, I would like to argue for Protestants—as I believe all sins are radically the same."

Father: "It is hardly worth while. You have only to take the judgment of all mankind, who in their laws and penalties distinguish sharply between petit and grand larceny, wounding and killing, and put you respectively in the jail or in the penitentiary, for a time or for life, and finally punish murder with death. Go on, Mr. Bee."

O. T. Bee: "You make, then, your resolution of amendment and foresee the means to be provided so you may keep it. Now you are ready for Confession and I expect Father had better take you in hand."

Father: "Excuse me, I would rather you should tell how you go about it. But you may all see from here the confessional door. Inside there is a kneeling bench, and between the penitent and priest a heavy grating, sometimes overspread for modesty's sake with a thick veil, as a priest need not recognize his penitents. The confessor sits as a Judge and a Father, to hear and decide, encourage and admonish—the penitent kneels as the accused and the accuser, and is taken at his word for good and ill. This is shown by the Father's first act in blessing his spiritual child at his express request: 'Father, bless me for I have sinned.'

" 'The Lord be in thy heart and upon thy lips that thou mayest confess well all thy sins, in the name † of the Father and of the Son and of the Holy Ghost.' Now, Mr. Bee."

O. T. Bee: "After the Confiteor, or some formula akin to it, you tell when you were at confession last, whether you received absolution and went to Holy Communion, and recite your sins in order—answering any questions the Father may ask to get a clearer idea of the state of your conscience. This done you wait for any advice against sinful habits or for attaining virtue and perfection the Father may give you, with the penance you have to say or perform."

Father: "Last comes the absolution, postponement or refusal, if dispositions and conditions are not such as to merit present forgiveness. Professor, you please translate the form."

Professor: "The priest, raising his right hand, says: 'May the Almigty God have mercy on thee, and forgive thee thy sins and bring thee into life everlasting. Amen. May the Almighty and merciful God grant thee pardon, † absolution and remission of thy sins. Amen.'

" 'May our Lord Jesus Christ absolve thee; and I, by His authority, do absolve thee from every bond of excommunication, (suspension—in case of priest's confession) and interdict, inasmuch as in my power lies, and thou dost stand in need. *Finally,* i absolve thee from thy sins, in the name of the Father † and of the Son, and of the Holy Ghost. Amen. May the Passion of our Lord Jesus Christ, the merits of the Blessed Virgin Mary and all the Saints, whatsoever good thou shalt have done and evil borne, be unto thee for the remission of sins, increase of grace, and reward of life everlasting. Amen.' "

Thomas: "Just in time to witness the procession for High Mass."

VII. PRESENTED TO THE DIVINE MAJESTY.

Father: "More solemn religious processions precede the Mass on High Feasts. In this part of the sacrifice called the Mass of the Catechumens and public penitents, who were excluded after the Gospel, we may converse in a low tone. There comes the cross bearer first, as the Bishop is present, succeeded by the Mass servers in red and purple cassocks and white surplices. Then masters of ceremonies, the archdeacon and deacon in gold cloth dalmatics, the celebrant in gold cloth chasuble—as this is the feast of Most Holy Trinity. And, finally, the assistants at the throne and the Rt. Rev. Bishop. There is a peaceful beauty in this simple procession, reminding us of the descriptions in the Old Testament and in St. John."

Professor: "I perceive the altar boys bowing to one another after the bending of the knee, and the clergy are doing the same before they part for their seats."

Father: "I see the drift of your remark. The

cremonies are a great school of mutual respect, and
even of decorum and politeness, whence no doubt
the civilizing influence descended into courts and
camps and found its way into society. The Church
is the conscious Mistress of all the refinements of
social intercourse, and tames by her example more,
perhaps, than by words. Now, as we shall not follow
the wording of the introduction of this sublime
drama, let us look on while I explain. Bear in mind
the pleasant discussion we had under yonder fine oak
when laying down the central idea of the Church
building. This is God's earthly palace, therefore
this is His Majesty's court on earth. All must focus
on this point. The Mass being the unbloody pre-
sentation of the Sacrifice of the Cross, in fact the
very continuation of it to the end of time for the
worship of God and the applying of our Savior's merits to souls, we must find in the very vestments traces
of His passion, death and resurrection—the priest
vesting and acting as the very Person of Christ. The
linen cloth, thrown upon the head of the priest and
lowered on his shoulders, represents the blindfolding
of our Lord; the long white garment or alb, his being clad in such a robe by Herod; the girdle, crossed
stole and maniple, the ropes used by the soldiers in
binding and haling Him to judgment; the chasuble
or outer vestment, the vari-colored or purple cloak
thrown over his shoulders; the priest's tonsure, His
crown of thorns."

Professor: "This sounds very much like the priest
pretended to act in the very person of our Lord. Can
this be so?"

Father: "Astonishing as it may seem it is the

truth. And this will convince you that the Church does nothing half way. As the celebrant acts out the character of our Lord, Jesus Christ, it need not surprise to hear the Catholic Armenians calling a priest's mother by the name of Our Lady, *Tiramajr*, mother of (our) Lord. Pause to note that the color of the vestments varies according to seasons and feasts. That the Apostles used such distinctions as separate costumes and colors for Mass, we infer from constant tradition and from regulations as far back as the time of St. Stephen I., 257 of our era. And if ancient vestments were somewhat similar to those in common use, in the period before Constantine and thence on to the fall of the Western Empire, the Church always retained her fashions and let the world follow its own. You know, Dr. Sam'l Johnson solemnly put it on record, that he thought the Mass the most venerable relic of antiquity the world possessed. So of the priestly garb—at least fifteen centuries old."

O. T. Bee: "But about the colors, Father?"

Father: "At the beginning of A. D. 300, white was already in use. And in 600 after Christ, St. Isidore records the introduction of red borders on white vestments.

"*White*, or gold and yellow, are used for the feasts of our Lord, B. Virgin, Angels, Virgins, etc.; *Red* at Pentecost--denoting fire—and festivals of Apostles and martyrs--denoting blood; *Violet* or purple, in seasons of penance; *Green*, the color of hope, on most other Sundays; and *Black*, or mourning *purple* in some instances, on Good Friday and at the Masses for the dead. Note, however, that it is never allowed to drape the altar or tabernacle in black; nor to have any signs of death on the palls or coverings of the chalice. Purple is used instead. The living and seeing God must be presented to us as He who was, is and ever shall be! Let men call our liturgy "mummeries" after that!"

Thomas: "The clergy have ascended the altar and the fuming censers are swinging."

Father: "Yes, but remark that you have just seen the same clergy bowing half-way to the floor and making their general confession to one another. This recalls the scene in the Garden of Olives, when our Lord lay prostrate and stricken, the victim for our sins and drinking the chalice of suffering to the bitter lees. The present motion of the celebrant, clothed in the garb resembling our Lord, pictures the haling before the High Priests and Pilate—and presently the changing, from the left to the right side of the altar, will reproduce the sending from Pilate to Herod and back again. The ministers incense the altar in token of the adoration of God by prayer. 'Let my prayer, O Lord, be directed as incense in thy sight,' said the prophet, King David."

Professor: "Any one who has read ancient history knows incense burning before altars was equivalent to worship."

Father: "Yes, and all the martyrs suffered death and the cruelest torture rather than submit to this act of worship before false gods or idols. It is chronicled of a youthful martyr, that upon his contemptuous refusal to adore a pagan deity, the enraged executioners forcibly held his hand, whose palm was filled with incense, over the flames, until the fire burned through the hero's palm and made the incense smoke.

They then triumphantly claimed the sainted child
had shown divine honor to the pitiable idol!"

Thomas· "I have often heard the objection to
having so many lighted candles."

Father: "I perceive your point. Only remember
that we were condemned to underground worship in
the catacombs and caves of the earth for the first
three hundred years, and lights were therefore a
simple necessity. We are sticklers for old fashions,
and hence have retained remembrances of those brave
old days. The very body of the altar recalls a bury-
ing place—the altar stone is the top slab—and in it
are inserted relics or bones of the saints, to make the
resemblance more tangible. This is one reason why
the priest kisses the altar at the middle. Then, are
not lights beautiful even in the daytime, and sym-
bolical of faith in our Lord, the light of the world
and the Love of our hearts? Besides, you scarcely
need reminding that we frequently have Masses at a
very early hour—it is allowed an hour before dawn—
and at Christmas, sometimes at midnight. Then we
have services after night as other people do.

"The sub-deacon is now singing the epistle, or por-
tion of Scripture selected to suit the feast, from the Let-
ters of the Apostles. He is but a Levite and serves the
celebrating minister. Behold how reverently he
carries the sacred Book and kneeling at the feet of
the priest receives his blessing and kisses his consecrated hand.

"While the priest reads the Gospel, or extracts
from one of the four Gospels, the Deacon or first
Levite prepares to solemnly sing the text, accompanied by all the inferior ministers, with tall candles

on each side, and the incense. All rise, even the Bishop, and hearken with utmost awe and attention to the word of God. Now the Book is carried to the Prelate, who kisses the page of the Gospel. Shouldn't all this prove in what esteem the Church holds the inspired writings? Why the higher ministers, from the sub-deacon up to the Pope, read every day for an hour or more, often an hour and a half, their Breviary, principally composed of the Scripture, relieved here and there with beautifully sententious hymns, and poetical prose antiphons, and the selected writings of the classic Christian authors."

Thomas: "More 'Father' tho', I imagine, than real Scripture, after all."

Father: "Think you so? You are egregiously and wildly mistaken, friend objector. The whole 150 psalms of David and other composers of the psaltery from the Jewish times, are read in the ferial office, *all over*, once a week—many psalms being repeated every day. And in the course of the year, the whole body of Scriptures, New and Old, with slight exceptions, are perused from end to end. Who of your ministers reads the whole Bible practically once every twelve months? And Monks and Nuns sing— sometimes for two hours to two and one-half hours— the major part of the office. Many millions of them arise in the dead of night to do this honor to the 'King of Ages,' and thus re-echo on earth the eternal praises never ceasing in the Court of the Highest Heaven!"

Lady Wilde: "Hark! they intone the sublime *Credo*—the Nicene, and if I remember rightly, the Constantinopolitan Creed. You will allow us to

join you in signing this Creed with both hands,
Father."

Father: "Aye, Madam, until we come to the 'One,
Holy, Catholic and Apostolic Church'—there we must
part, eh?"

Lady Wilde: "Why, no, sir. We subscribe that
too. It is the glory of the Church of England
Branch."

Father: "Ah! the Church of England! But not
the one universal and united Catholic Church. England is not universal—the Church is.

"But now they are nearing the close of the less sacred
part of the Sacrifice, the prologue to the Holiest
Drama the world ever witnessed. Permit me to kneel
and merely translate—with the Professor looking on
—from the Offertory. This is so called for the double
reason that the elements of bread and wine are first
offered and blessed, and that on certain occasions
offerings of bread, wine, the fruits of the earth and
firstlings of crops were formerly presented and
blessed near the altar. The scene of the sentence
passed on our Lord is also here represented.

THE OFFERTORY.

"I wish to emphasize the remark that this MASS OF
THE MOST HOLY TRINITY, is the identical Sacrifice of
Thanksgiving ordered by Leo XIII. for the Church in
Italy, Spain, Portugal and the two Americas, on
Columbus Day, Oct. 21, 1892.

"'Blessed be the Holy Trinity and the undivided
Unity: We shall praise Him, because He hath shown
His mercy unto us. Ps. 8. Lord, our Lord, how
wondrous is Thy name in all the earth!'"

"The Host, in the form of a flat round wafer of
pure flour and water, typifying our Lord's innocence,
is then offered on the gold paten, as Jesus offered
himself as a victim,

" 'Accept, O Holy Father, Almighty, Everlasting God, this stainless Host, which I, Thy unworthy servant, offer unto Thee, my God, living and true, for my innumerable sins, offences, and shortcomings, and for all here present; as also for all faithful Christians, both living and dead, that it may be profitable for my own and their salvation unto life eternal. *Amen*.'

"We may note the remarkable ceremony observed in Catholic countries, in the Netherlands principally, and in connection more especially with solemn requiems. Just preceding these prayers the congregation pass one by one up to the communion rail, where the deacon presents the back of the paten to be kissed. The uninterrupted motion of the ministers pictures the surging of the Jewish priests, scribes, Levites and rabble on the way to Golgotha. The sub-deacon hands the wine and water to the deacon, who pours about an ounce of wine mingled with a few drops of water into the chalice, while the priest blesses the water in these words: *

'O God, † who hast wonderfully founded man's dignified nature, and still more wonderfully reformed it; grant us, by the significant commingling of this water and wine, to become partakers of His Godhead who hath deigned to become partaker of our manhood, Jesus Christ, Thy Son, our Lord; who liveth and reigneth with Thee in the unity of, etc. *Amen*.'

Giving the gold paten to the sub-deacon to hold wrapped in the veil till after the Pater Noster, the deacon kisses the foot of the chalice and the hand of the priest as he hands it him, saying with the celebrant:

'We-offer to Thee, O Lord, the chalice of salvation, beseeching Thy sweet mercy that, in the sight of

---

* Wherever this sign of the cross † appears in the liturgy, the celebrant forms the same holy symbol with hi. 'ght hand as he blesses the object.

Thy divine Majesty, it may ascend with the savor of sweetness, for our salvation, and that of the whole world. *Amen.*'

Bowing down—imitating Christ in receiving His sentence of death from Pilate—the priest says:

'In an humble spirit and a contrite heart may we be received by thee, O Lord; and let our Sacrifice be such in Thy sight to-day that it may please Thee, O Lord God.'

Suddenly standing erect, to show his dignity as mediator and thus imitating his master, by a sublime change from the posture of humility he invokes the Lord God of Israel, as Elijah did before the four hundred priests of Baal:

'Come, O Sanctifier, Almighty, Eternal God, and bless † this sacrifice set ready unto Thy holy name.'

Follows the solemn incensing of the table of the altar, the relics between the candle-sticks, the crucifix, and the front and ends of the altar, the priest blessing incense thus:

'By the intercession of blessed Michael the Archangel, standing at the right hand of the Altar of Incense, and of all His elect, may the Lord be pleased to bless this incense, and receive it as an odor of sweetness. Through, etc. *Amen.*

Fuming the elements of bread and wine triply in the form of a cross, and triply in the form of a circle, he says:

'May this incense which Thou hast blessed, O Lord, ascend to Thee, and may Thy mercy descend upon us.'

These are the poetical and beautiful extracts from the psalms he recites as he swings the censer—very similarly to the priests incensing in the Old Law.

'Let my prayer, O Lord, be directed as incense in Thy sight: and the lifting up of my hands as the evening sacrifice.

Set a watch, O Lord, before my mouth; keep a door round about my lips.

Lest my heart may incline to evil words, to frame excuses in sins.'

Handing the thurible to the Deacon, who presently incenses him—the Rt. Rev. Bishop and Clergy, the Sub-deacon and people—the Priest says:

'May the Lord enkindle in us the fire of His love, and the flame of everlasting charity. *Amen*.

Declining to the epistle side of the Altar the celebrant commemorates the laving of Pilate's hands, when he declared he was guiltless of the blood of Jesus, by washing his fingers, as he quotes the conclusion of Psalm 25th:

'I will wash my hands among the innocents; and I will compass Thine altar, O Lord.

That I may hear the voice of praise, and tell of all Thy wondrous works.

O Lord, I have loved the beauty of Thy house, and the place where Thy glory dwelleth.

Make not my soul, O God, perish with the wicked, nor my life with men of blood.

In whose hands are iniquities; their right hand is filled with bribes.

But as for me, I have entered, in my innocence: redeem me, and be merciful unto me.

My foot hath stood in the right way: in the churches I will bless Thee, O Lord.

Glory be to the Father, etc.'

Returning to the middle of the alter, he recites this solemn oblation—plainly intimating the close connection of the unbloody sacrifice with the Passion of our Lord:

'Receive, O Holy Trinity, this Oblation, which we offer to Thee, in memory of the Passion, Resurrection, and Ascension of our Lord Jesus Christ, and in honor of blessed Mary Ever-Virgin, of blessed

John the Baptist, of the holy Apostles Peter and Paul, of these and all Thy Saints; that it may avail to their honor and our salvation; and may they vouchsafe to intercede for us in heaven, whose memory we celebrate on earth. Through the same Christ our Lord. *Amen.*'

Imitating the placing of our Lord, with his purple vestment and crown of thorns, before the people by Pilate's order, as the Governor exclaimed: Ecce Homo! Behold the man; the Priest turns to the congregation, saying:

'Pray, my brethren, that my sacrifice and yours may be made acceptable to God the Father Almighty.'

Which the servers, in the name of the people, and in contrast to the saying of the Jews—'Crucify Him'—answer:

'May the Lord receive the Sacrifice from thy hands, to the praise and glory of His name, for our benefit, and that of all His holy Church.'

The procession in Jerusalem to hurry our Lord to Calvary is here represented as starting. Presently a procession of servers with lights at the Sanctus will typify it. The Way of the Cross is scenically recalled by the rising of the dignitaries and people at the Preface.

After the prayer or prayers called 'Collects,' surrounded by all the attendants in picturesque grouping, while the Bishop and Clergy rise with the congregation, the celebrant ends the last petition with: 'Thro' our Lord Jesus Christ, who liveth and reigneth with the Father and the Holy Ghost,' singing: 'World without end.'

'*R.* Amen. *V.* The Lord be with you. *R.* And with thy spirit. *V.* Uplift your hearts. *R.* We lift them up unto the Lord. *V.* Let us give thanks to the Lord our God. *R.* It is worthy and just.'

Ensues the preface or prelude to the Canon, the most sacred part of the Liturgy—in such music as Mozart confessed he would have given all his honors to be able to equal.

'It is truly meet and just, proper and profitable unto salvation, that we should at all times and in all places give thanks unto Thee, O Holy Lord, Father Almighty, Eternal God. Who, with Thine Only-begotten Son and the Holy Ghost, art one God, art one Lord: not in the singleness of one only Person, but in the Trinity of one Substance. For what we believe of Thy glory, as Thou hast revealed it, that we firmly hold, of Thy Son, that of the Holy Ghost, without any difference or inequality. That in the confession of the True and Eternal Godhead, distinction in Persons, unity in Essence, and equality in Majesty may be adored. Whom the Angels and Archangels, the Cherubim and Seraphim, together praise; who cease not daily to cry out, with one voice.' * * *

This is the form of the preface sung on Trinity Sundays and on ordinary Sundays. There are, including those chanted at the Blessing of Palms and the Blessing of the Paschal Candle and of the Font, on Holy Saturday and the Eve of Pentecost, thirteen varied Prefaces. At the Sanctus the bell is rung thrice and all kneel.

'Holy, Holy, Holy, Lord God of Hosts. Heavens and earth are full of Thy glory. Hosanna in the highest. Blessed is he who cometh in the name of the Lord. Hosanna in the highest.'

VIII THE CANON OF THE MASS.

(With the two Ministers standing on either side, the Priest raises hands and eyes to heaven and continues in a low voice—which he keeps up till the Pater Noster).

'We, therefore, humbly pray and beseech Thee, most merciful Father, through Jesus Christ Thy Son, our Lord '

(Kissing the altar he gives a triple blessing to the Host and Chalice—praying).

'That Thou wouldst accept and bless these † gifts, these † presents, these· † holy unspotted sacrifices, which, in the first place, we offer Thee for Thy Holy Catholic Church; to which vouchsafe to grant peace, guard, unite, and govern throughout the whole world, together with Thy servant N. our Pope; N. our Bishop; as also all orthodox believers and professors of the Catholic and Apostolic Faith.'

Next is made the special and general Memento of the Living, or the Intention of the Mass. It is to obtain this peculiar privilege of having their personal petitions united with the adorable sacrifice that the faithful give the Priest a stipend or alms—not of course to buy the priceless boon of the Mass, but to contribute towards the celebrant's and altar's support.

'Remember, O Lord, Thy servants and handmaids, N. and N., And all present, whose faith and devotion well Thou knowest; for whom we offer, or who offer up to Thee this Sacrifice of praise for themselves and all theirs, for the redemption of their souls, for the hope of their safety and well-being, and who pay their vows unto Thee, the eternal God, living and true.'

To portray in a lively manner the union of the three divisions of the Church, Militant on Earth, Suffering in Purgatory and Triumphant in Heaven,

*

then follows the declaratory prayer, which is varied on the highest festivals, Christmas, Epiphany, Easter, Ascension and Pentecost.

'In the company, and honoring the memory, especially of the glorious Ever-Virgin Mary, Mother of our God and Lord Jesus Christ; as also of Thy blessed Apostles and Martyrs, Peter and Paul, Andrew, James, John, Thomas, James, Philip. Bartholomew, Matthew, Simon and Thaddeus, Linus, Cletus, Clement, Xystus, Cornelius, Cyprian, Lawrence, Chrysogonus, John and Paul, Cosmas and Damian, and all Thy Saints; by whose merits and prayers grant that we may in all things be shielded by the aid of Thy protection. Through the same Christ our Lord. *Amen.*'

(*In whisper.*) The organ is silent. Prepare for the Consecration—or words of Christ by which the substance of the bread and wine, the outward form and appearances remaining unchanged—is changed into the substance of the real, true Body and Blood of Jesus Christ. As the priests spreads his hands over the elements, the bell is rung once.

'This oblation, therefore, of our service, and indeed of Thy whole family, we beseech Thee, O Lord, graciously to accept; and to dispose our days in Thy peace, and to command us to be delivered from eternal damnation, and let us be numbered in the flock of Thine elect. Through Christ our Lord. *Amen.*

Which oblation do Thou, O God, we beseech Thee, vouchsafe to make all things blessed, † approved, † ratified, † reasonable, and acceptable; that it may be made for us the Body † and Blood † of Thy dearly beloved Son, our Lord Jesus Christ.

Who, the day before He suffered, took bread into His holy and venerable hands, and with eyes lifted up towards heaven, unto Thee, O God, His Almighty Father, giving thanks to Thee, did bless, † break, and give unto His disciples, saying: Take, and eat ye all of this.'

(Following strictly the action of our Lord in consecrating or saying Holy Mass at the Last Supper, the celebrant takes the Host in his hands, lifts eyes to heaven, blesses, [and presently breaks the Host in three parts, and distributes communion,] and says secretly, but distincty, the Divine Words:)

"FOR THIS IS MY BODY."

(Suiting the action to the words, he pursues speaking, and doing as if the actual person of the Son of God.)

'In like manner, after supper, taking also this excellent chalice into His holy and venerable hands; and giving thanks to Thee, He blessed, † and gave to His disciples, saying: Take, and drink ye all of it.'

(Leaning over the chalice slightly bent towards him, he pronounces the sacred formula:)

' "FOR THIS IS THE CHALICE OF MY BLOOD OF THE NEW AND ETERNAL TESTAMENT: THE MYSTERY OF FAITH: WHICH SHALL BE SHED FOR YOU, AND FOR MANY, UNTO THE REMISSION OF SINS.' "

' "As often as ye do these things, ye shall do them in remembrance of Me.' "

Notice, he and all present who were standing, kneel twice at each elevation of the Host and Chalice--the celebrant, where the Blessed Sacrament is not reserved previously in the tabernacle, not having hitherto bent the knee, since the very beginning of the Holy Sacrifice.

'Wherefore, O Lord, we Thy servants, and likewise Thy holy people, calling to mind the blessed Passion of the same Christ Thy Son, our Lord, together with His Resurrection from the grave, and also His glorious Ascension into heaven, offer unto Thy most excellent Majesty, of Thy gifts and presents, a pure † Victim, a holy † Victim, an immaculate † Victim, the holy † bread of eternal life, and the chalice † of everlasting salvation.'

The elevation representing the raising of our Lord crucified on the wood of sacrifice, our Lord's body and the chalice containing His precious blood are held aloft for the adoration of the faithful. The five wounds are typified by these last five signs of the Cross.

(*Extending his hands to image the stretching of our Lord's arms on the Cross—or really putting out both arms in the shape of a Cross, as the older Liturgies direct, and the Dominicans still practice*).

'Upon which do Thou vouchsafe to look with favorable and serene countenance, and accept them, as Thou didst vouchsafe to accept the gifts of Thy just servant Abel, and the sacrifice of our Patriarch Abraham, and that which Thy High-priest Melchisedech offered unto Thee, a holy Sacrifice, an unspotted Victim.'

(*Bowing down his forehead nearly to his joined hands on the Altar, kissing the spot adjoining the front edge of the Corporal, raising his head erect and blessing the Sacred Species and himself*).

'We humbly beseech Thee, Almighty God, command these to be carried by the hands of Thy holy Angel to Thine Altar on high, in the sight of Thy divine Majesty, that as many of us as shall, by partaking at this Altar, receive the most sacred Body † and Blood † of Thy Son, may be filled with every heavenly blessing and grace. Through the same Christ our Lord. *Amen.*'

Memento or Intention by name for the dead, in which also the faithful may obtain the special mention of departed relatives, friends or of some specific class of souls, or finally all the souls in purgatory:

'Remember, O Lord, Thy servants and handmaids, N. and N., who are gone before us with the sign of faith, and sleep the sleep of peace.'

'To these, O Lord, and to all who rest in Christ, grant, we pray Thee, a place of refreshment, light and peace. Through the same Christ our Lord. *Amen.*'

These and accompanying prayers and actions give token of the realization of the Passion. Striking his breast, as in the following, he recalls the act of individuals at the Passion when they repented of sin—and many fled in terror at the darkness fallen on Calvary:

'To us also, Thy sinful servants, hoping in the multitude of Thy mercies, vouchsafe to grant some part and fellowship with Thy holy Apostles and Martyrs; with John, Stephen, Matthias, Barnabas, Ignatius, Alexander, Marcellinus, Peter, Felicitas, Perpetua, Agatha, Lucy, Agnes, Cecilia, Anastasia, and all Thy Saints; into whose company, not weighing our merits, but freely pardoning our offences, we beseech Thee to admit us. Through Christ our Lord.

By whom, O Lord, Thou dost always create, sanctify, † quicken, † bless, † and present to us all these good things.'

(*The Minor Elevation, which ensues, consists in making five signs of the Cross again, over and in front of the Chalice with the Sacred Host itself, at the end of which he raises the Chalice with his left hand while he supports his right hand by holding the Host over the cup*):

'Through Him, † and with Him, † and in Him, † is to Thee, God the Father † Almighty, in the unity of the Holy † Ghost, all honor and glory.'

The Drama of the Cross is so real that here are represented, in the OUR FATHER's seven petitions, the seven distinct utterances of the dying Master, during His three hours' agony: Finishing the minor elevation the priest sings:

'V. World without end. R. Amen.

THE PATER NOSTER.

Let us pray.

'Admonished by Thy saving precepts, and follow
ing Thy divine instruction, we make bold to say:
Our Father, who art in heaven, hallowed be Thy
name: Thy kingdom come: Thy will be done on
earth as it is in heaven. Give us this day our daily
bread: and forgive us our trespasses, as we forgive
those who trespass against us. And lead us not into
temptation. R. But deliver us from evil. P. Amen.'

*(Here the subdeacon, who has been holding wrapped
in the ends of the veil the paten, brings it to the deacon,
who, unfolding the veil, presents the paten, after kissing it and the hand of the priest, who pursues:)*

'Deliver us, we beseech Thee, O Lord, from all
evils, past, present, and future: and by the intercession of blessed and glorious Mary Ever-Virgin,
Mother of God, together with Thy blessed Apostles
Peter and Paul, and Andrew, and all the Saints,'—

*(Making the sign of the cross on himself with the
paten, which he also kisses and places under the Sacred
Host.)*

Graciously give peace in our days: that, aided by
the help of Thy mercy, we may be always free from
sin, and secure from all disturbances,'—

*(Breaking the Sacred Species of Bread in two, and
then a particle off the lower edge of one-half.)*

'Through the same our Lord Jesus Christ, Thy Son,
Who liveth and reigneth with Thee in the unity of
the Holy Ghost, God. V. World without end. R.
Amen.

*(Making a triple sign with particle over the cup he
deposits it in the Sacred Blood. Showing the death of
our Lord and the descent of His soul into Limbo.)*

'V. May the peace † of the Lord be † always with
† you. R. And with thy spirit. May this commingling

and consecration of the Body and Blood of our Lord Jesus Christ be unto us that receive it effectual to life everlasting. Amen.'

The humble posture of the Celebrant, assistants and whole people, together with the striking of the breast three times, at the Agnus Dei, and directly at the Communion, reminds of the similar act of the multitude at Mt. Calvary, when our Lord died:

'Lamb of God, who takest away the sins of the world, have mercy on us. Lamb of God, who takest away the sins of the world, have mercy on us. Lamb of God, who takest away the sins of the world, grant us peace.'

'O Lord Jesus Christ, who saidst to Thine Apostles, Peace I leave you, My peace I give unto you: regard not my sins, but the faith of thy Church; and vouchsafe to it that peace and unity which is agreeable to Thy will: who livest and reignest God world without end. Amen.'

The touching embrace the Celebrant gives the deacon and the latter communicates to the subdeacon, who in turn carries the Kiss of Peace to all others, enacts over again the salutation at the *Agapes* or Love-feasts of Christians in early ages, in conjunction with the reception of Holy Communion—the Bond of Faith, of Love and Peace:

'V. Peace be with thee.   R. And with thy spirit.'

The priest finishes the Communion prayer, now entirely proper to himself, as the most special fruit of the Sacrifice is applied for his own santification.

'O Lord Jesus Christ, Son of the Living God, who, according to the will of the Father and the co-operation of the Holy Ghost, hast by Thy death given life to the world: deliver me by this Thy most sacred Body and Blood from all my iniquities and from all evils; and make me always adhere to Thy commandments, and suffer me never to be parted from Thee. Who

with the same God the Father and the Holy Ghost
livest and reignest God world withòut end.   Amen,
Let not the partaking of Thy Body, O Lord Jesus
Christ, which I, unworthy, as I am, presume to receive,
turn to my judgment and condemnation; but by Thy
mercy be it profitable to the safety and health both of
soul and body.   Who with God the Father, in the
unity of the Holy Ghost, livest and reignest God
world without end.   Amen.'

(*Genuflecting, rising and taking the broken Host and
paten in his left hand, plainly figuring the broken body
of Christ, whom he is in a moment to enshrine in his
breast:*)

'I will take the Bread of heaven, and will call upon
the name of the Lord.'

(*Striking his breast thrice, as he leans forward:*)

'Lord, I am not worthy that Thou shouldst enter
under my roof; but only say the word, and my soul
shall be healed.'

(*Receiving reverently on his tongue—to let It dissolve
there and swallow—he communicates himself—first making with the Host the sign of the Holy Cross:*)

'May the Body of our Lord Jesus Christ preserve
my soul unto life everlasting.   Amen.'

(*Collecting carefully every minutest crumb fallen
from the Sacred Host—the 'precious pearls', as the East-
ern Liturgy calls them, he deposits them in the Chalice
of Blood.*)

'What shall I return unto the Lord for all the
things that he hath rendered unto me?   I will take
the chalice of salvation, and call upon the name of
the Lord.   I will call upon the Lord and give praise:
and I shall be saved from mine enemies.'

(*Consuming the Sacred Blood to the last fragment of
a drop—making the sign of the Cross with Chalice before he puts it to his lips.*)

'May the Blood of our Lord Jesus Christ preserve
my soul unto life everlasting. Amen.'

*(In the Communion of the faithful, under the form of
Bread only, as our Lord is wholly present under each
form and each particle of each form, when separated,
the absolution follows.)*

'May Almighty God have mercy upon you, and
forgive you your sins, and bring you unto life everlasting.· R. Amen. May the Almighty and merciful Lord grant you pardon, † absolution, and remission of your sins.'

*(Turning with the Sacred Particle elevated over the
Ciborium he warns the faithful in the words of John the
Baptist)*:

'Behold the Lamb of God, behold Him who taketh
away the sins of the world.'

*(Then three times repeating the humble protestation of the
Centurion, to whom our Lord went to cure his servant—only
substituting 'soul' for 'servant.')* ·

'Lord, I am not worthy that Thou shouldst enter
under my roof; but only say the word, and my soul
shall be healed.'

*(Feeding the pious communicant with his priestly hand, he
uses the formula)*:

'The body of our Lord Jesus Christ preserve thy
soul unto life everlasting. *Amen.*'

*(Washing the chalice, first with a modicum of wine.
then cleansing his fingers over the cup, he says)*:

'What we have taken with our mouth, O Lord, may
we receive with a pure mind; and of a temporal gift
may it become to us an everlasting remedy. May
Thy Body, O Lord, which I have received, and Thy
Blood which I have drunk, cleave unto my inmost
parts; and grant that no stain of sin may remain in
me, who have been refreshed with pure and holy
Sacraments. Who livest, etc. *Amen.*'

And the Sacrifice proper is accomplished. In the remaining acts, presenting himself with outstretched hands to the people, and finally blessing them and disappearing, the Priest personates the apparitions of the Savior after the Resurrection and at last His Ascension, as He blesses all His disciples.

BOOKLET III.—VALUE OF THE CHURCH
IN DOLLARS AND CENTS.

——— —

I. SOME ROLLING STOCK.

———

SCENE—LOURDWELL AVENUE IN SIGHT OF VILLA ST.
LAWRENCE.

———

CHARACTERS:

Thomas Objector,   Professor,
O. T. Bee,   Father,
        Uncommercial Traveler.

···············

Professor: "Well, Father and gentlemen, I am
fond of serious study; but I am also of the opinion
that in the popular expressive phrase, it is time 'to
let up,' and 'give us a rest.'"

Father: "Exactly my idea. We have adjourned
to this fine sylvan retreat to discuss lightly what we
may call the 'Financial After-piece,' after our labors
of dissecting the sects and poring over the superb
Liturgy."

O. T. Bee, Uncom. Traveler, Thomas Objector—
(In chorus): "Controversy avaunt! Something
now on which all minds of money-getting Americans
agree."

Father: "Let us raise a head of steam' and com-
pute the value of the rolling-stock of the SHORT LINE

—that is, calculate roughly, what commercial interests are served by the existence and continuance of the Catholic Church in this Republic. For, mind, we are going back rarely to musty old times or foreign countries for facts and figures.

Uncom. Traveler: "For the sake of contradiction, I will take the side of the old Know-Nothings, aye, and the new loud-mouthed associations, which have for their object the overthrow of the Catholic religion here. I say then (rather serio-comicall), that I would like to side and work with these 'patriots,' to burn all your churches and schools, smash your idolatrous pictures and church furniture—and wipe out every vestige of everything Catholic and strangle every mother's son of a Catholic —— "

Father—(*Smiling knowingly*): "You would make an ideal iconoclast. But I will take you at your word. Suppose everybody Catholic dead or banished; everything Catholics use a heap of smoking ruins! And, if you like, figure to yourself the Grand Master of the What-you-call-it, standing on the top of the rubbish, proclaiming with a wave of his flag America's eternal freedom from 'popery,' with all its works and pomps. Reckon up now the good that would result to America from such a glorious Revolution, as that of France a century ago, demolishing and annihilating Catholicity. How would it affect trade? First, it would bless the Republic with a clear lessening of its population by one-sixth, or ten million souls—Some say, twelve or thirteen millions."

Traveler: "Out with them! They're a beggarly lot, ha! ha!"

Father: "Catholics are mostly artisans, trades-people and agriculturists; few rich. The deprivation of surely 3,000,000 working people would be a signal boon for the industries of the country.''

Thomas: "Hold on! You are too modest. It would be at least a million more than that. Your 10,000,000 would represent 2,000,000 families, and you are counting but one and a half wage-earners to a family.''

Father: "I stand corrected; say 4,000,000. Add to these 1,000,000 Catholic children, who are calculated as going to the public schools, which, of course, would be glad to be rid of them, and of the taxes paid by 2,500,000 poll-heads to the National and State funds.''

Uncom. Traveler: "Humph! I doubt that. These children represent at least 1000 to 1200 schools, and 2800 to 3000 teachers who would be thrown out of employment.''

Father: "Oho! So you imagine this kind of blessing would be 'over the left!' We count tho' just about as many human beings, by the 5,000,000 knocked out of trade and school, as there were soldiers from first to last engaged in the late civil war. By the way, how would it affect the army and navy?''

O. T. Bee: "I have had occasion to study statistics of our forces on land and water, and little short of half of them are computed as Catholics.''

Father: "Just so; it would cut the defense of the country half in two. By the way, do you remember seeing the proofs not long ago unearthed, from an inquiry in the then sitting House of Commons, that about 'half the rebel continental army' under Washington, 'were from Ireland;' and these, with all the

Navy under the French, were rank 'Papists.' And
while I have this little thread of history in my hand,
I dare assert to Americans that, looking over the map
of the United States, all the territory now covered by
thirty-four organized and unorganized commonwealths, was discovered and originally settled by two
Catholic powers; the very powers, by the way, which
first recognized our independence."

Professor: "That is a bold and broad assertion.
But, withal, I believe you can substantiate it. I suppose you refer to France and Spain. Less than half
of the original thirteen colonies on the Atlantic sea-
board were first taken possession of or acquired by
England—Massachusetts, Rhode Island and New
Hampshire, Virginia, Georgia and perhaps Tennessee. Oh! yes, throw in Utah—colonized by Anglo-
Saxon 'saints.' "

Father: "Concede seven others to Holland,
Sweden, Scotland—though you have to add Ireland in
Pennsylvania and half the Carolinas—and we still
prove claim to the primitive possession and explora-
tion of 34 States and Territories. The sign of
Christ's cross is over them all—'a soil,' asserverates
Card. Gibbons, 'fertilized by the blood and sweat of
Catholic explorers, founders and missionaries'—and
that over a century before the Salem plantation. But,
ah! we have been betrayed into a page of history,
despite our protest. It does look tho' as if a handful
of newcomers were trying to evict the oldest inhabitants. By my priest's cap, if this land belonged *first*
to the roving and scattered Indian tribes, it assuredly
belonged, *secondly*, to France and Spain; and only
thirdly, to these great United States!"

Thomas: "Well, now, let's have some more sums in addition. We had 5,000,000—the men and wageworkers averaging, say, $300 worth apiece, $1,500,-000,000; the children, counting in the 800,000 in Catholic schools and 500,000 others of school age either married or not at school, 1,300,000 altogether, worth prospectively at least $100 apiece—tho' now costing something—would aggregate $130,000,000. The total for the present would amount to the left-handed blessing of the loss to the country of the sum of $1,430,000,000—nearly a billion and a half of dollars! That would double the whole National debt and bring it back to war figures. Look here, Father, this is getting 'too steep.' "

Father: "Are not the figures very moderate? And are they eminently correct? But this is nothing like the grand total. Add to your sum the over $118,-381,516, which the U. S. census report says our Catholic institutions were worth two years ago. Put down besides, that we have on the Pacific coast alone, our 'few rich and noble' ten years ago:

J. W. Mackay, worth	$150,000,000
Jas. C. Flood, worth	68,000,000
J. G. Fair, worth	50,000,000
L. Coleman, worth	50,000,000
Peter Donohoe, worth	25,000,000
Hugh McGuire, worth	20,000,000
C. E. Crocker (Pratt), worth	20,000,000
Luke Cavanaugh, worth	15,000,000
Gerald Malone, worth	12,000,000
W. I. O'Reilly, worth	8,000,000
Farther East, at least 10 more worth	82,000,000

Thomas : "Just $720,000,000. Grand total so far: Two billions, one-hundred and sixty-eight millions, three hundred and eighty-one thousand, five hundred and sixteen dollars—$2,168,381,516! ! !''

O. T. Bee: "By Jove, I'm getting enthusiastic over my religion. If that grand total at present were withdrawn from circulation, it would suspend half our banks, bankrupt 20,000 firms, and give such a blow to trade that the minority of the working population and thousands of capitalists would be brought to the brink of ruin. Wall street ——''

Father: "Hold on, Mr. Bee, we know all that. Besides, it is no credit to you to be proud of your faith when you neglect its practice precisely on account of the almighty dollar. In another sense, it is no harm to boast of the temporal good and profit the church indirectly confers on the republic—as Pope Leo quotes from St. Augustin: 'The faith of Christ indirectly benefits as materially as if it had been instituted for that purpose.' Meanwhile, let the native Americans or kindred revolutionary societies put that 168 millions over two billions of dollars in their pipes and smoke it—roll it around in their pockets and feel how big it is, until we give them more to do. How does stock in the SHORT LINE stand now?''

II. CONTINGENT EXPENSES.

Father: "Professor, I am sorry we can't debate for your benefit and with your educated help, the enormous advantage the existence and maintenance of the Catholic Church in our midst brings to the commonwealths of this Union, on the score of the civilization it imparts in its schools, churches, home and society in general."

Professor, (*laughing*). "Yes, I confess your money question isn't very interesting to me personally. I would rather have a whack at your stand on the purity of the ballot, for example; on your care of the poor, sick, the soldier, the hunted Indian and the still downtrodden negro. Most of all I would enjoy the discussion of the church's doctrine and practice regarding marriage, divorce and ——"

Father: "Well, gentlemen, I believe we can gratify the professor and the broad-minded and well-read public, in this very following division of the dollar and cent aspect of the Old Church. I refer to the question: What loss in population, money, progress and enlightenment this country would suffer, say, in the next generation—supposing everything and everybody Catholic were suddenly uprooted from our soil?"

Professor: "It is proved beyond cavil that your church members form the fastest multiplying body in America. Why, I remember that ten years ago, your conservative advocates claimed only 7,000,000 in the United States—and now you are at least one-half more numerous. This is 50 per cent. gain in a decade."

Uncom. Traveler: "I remember reading on the train one of your recent Catholic Truth Society pamphlets by Card. Gibbons, in which he asserts, that 100 years ago you Catholics counted but 32,000 or 1-107th of the population. I saw too, indeed, that the Germans and Irish from over the water contributed nearly half your figures up to our Centennial year."

Father: "*Young* emigrants from Italy, Poland and Hungary have increased of late until they surpass the

Irish or German new-comers. All these, together
with the birth-rate among Catholics, will undoubted-
ly double our population by the next generation—say
in 1925. Do figures in official statistics bear me out
in that assertion and prophecy, Professor?"

Professor: "I am sure they do. If Catholics form
already half or nearly the half of our citizens in New
York City and Boston (bless the mark!) and a large
third in Philadelphia, St. Louis, (not to add Chicago)
Cincinnati, Milwaukee and Louisville, exactly because of the sanctity of Catholic marriage-ties; there
is no reason to doubt that the still healthier population of the country, for instance in Maryland, Louis-
iana, Minnesota, are more prolific in proportion."

Father: "Now—I beg pardon for the interruption—
the argument I want to make is precisely this: If the
withdrawal of the mass of Catholics, in this Union, has
been cleverly and modestly calculated as sufficient to
knock the bottom out of the circulation of over two
thousand millions ot dollars—who can estimate what
trillions of losses will result from an absence from the
country of a creed boasting a following, which, in a
single third of a century, will develop itself into
25,000,000 people?"

Uncom. Traveler: "But don't you 'bank' more
largely on the foreigners than on your native birth-
rate?"

Father: "Thomas, I'll let you answer that?"

Thomas: "If Traveler means by foreigners such as
were born in European countries, I can show him, in
the *Washington Sentinel*, official tables of 1870, that there
were, in the decade 1870 and 1880, not more than
4,000,000 left then of the English Puritan stock—*with*

an ever decreasing birth-rate—whilst other nationalities and their descendants (of course excluding the negro freed men) rolled up nearly to 24,500,000—with a birth-rate *3 1-5 times as great* in proportion as the what is called 'pure native stock.' Advancing, however, to 1880 and 1890, in justice we have to count, *as natives*, the enormous increase of population born here of parents coming from Europe. The law esteems them as such, and one such might be even president of the United States. But then, add to this that there are great mistakes made in supposing that the majority of the Catholic element in the country are in any sense foreigners or children of foreigners, unless all the inhabitants of the country--outside of the native Indians--are accounted as such. I know that the great majority of Catholics in, for instance, Kentucky, Maryland, are originally English stock; that now six millions out of our ten millions, at least, are estimated as *native-born*. In the two states above, in Indiana, Tennessee, Kansas, Texas and Arkansas, the census figures of 1880 only summed up about 450,000 foreign-born citizens.''

Father: ''Now, sirs, I think it is lawful to conclude that we don't 'bank' principally on foreigners--and that our 25,000,000 in 1925, will be composed mainly of just as good native Americans as you can scare up!''

III.   HOW'S TRADE IF WE DO STAY ?

Father: ''But, gentlemen, there is another and more agreeable aspect of the case. We Catholics are

here, to stay, and what is more, nobody but some car-
lots of lazy, penniless and blatant 'gas-bags' want to
part with us. Our interests are all interwoven insep-
arably in the maintenance of this best republic God
ever blessed earth with, and in the weal and prosperity
of every freeman on the soil. Now, how does the
Catholic church affect the advancements of the arts
and sciences? How does she help to run the country's
trade and pour money into the laps of industrious
citizens of all classes? Poetry, music, painting,
sculpture, architecture--which one of the fine arts is
a stranger to her; or rather, who can prove that she
is not a most open-handed, constant and intelligent
patron of each one separately and of all conjointly?
These are questions for the leaders of thought."

Thomas—"Very good! We are about as well-posted
leaders of thought as we can conveniently gather.
Let me object that the Catholics of the country are
generally of the poorer and uneducated classes; and
therefore, the church composed of them can be no
munificent patron of the arts?"

Father: "There, professor, there is a nut for you
to crack. I don't like common walnuts."

Professor: "Not very creditable to the objector!
But that is exactly the wonder to me; how your poor
people can be gotten to raise such costly and magnificent temples, while we of the other denominations
can generally, with all our wealthy members, imitate
you afar off, and never equal, much less surpass you."

Father: "That is easily solved. The wage-earners
are often more liberal than your aristocrats, and in
the case of Catholics there is such a spur of religion,
conscience, other-world sense, that they give freely,

frequently, and in such numbers that the prelates and pastors, who are public-spirited, can do wonders.

"Of course, I need only allude to the cathedrals of Boston, Hartford, Providence, right in the heart of Yankeedom, and where our people seem to have started the worst equipped, both in purse and brains, to illustrate what enormously expensive public works we carry on, and how elegantly, artistically they are wrought

I have lately seen and examined the details of the two latter cathedrals, and more varied, imposing and richer treasure-houses of the whole circle of arts they contain it is hard to find in the land. Their architecture is of the boldest, carrying out in modern stone, iron and marble and brass and stucco, the dreams of the master-builders of the ages of the best Gothic and Renaissance. Listen to the harmony that breathes from the acanthus-capped pillars, the delicate tracery of the groining, the marbled walls, the life-picturing stained glass, the precious altars and storied niches of saints; and the figures, angelic and human, standing out from canvas and panelling. Does it need to hear the organ swell thro' the nave and be answered by the chancel, alive and moving now in the poetic liturgy, to perceive here an embodiment of all the muses, in all the divine glamour of the heavenly, reflected in the religious 'pomp and circumstance' of peace!

Indeed, it is to break a dream and be snagged on the hard thorns of life, to ask: How much all this is worth in dollars and cents? But a trading people will ask it and calculate its worth to the community. How much educated and exquisite talent has been bought and expended on these mounting pinnacles, soaring domes, gilded frescoes, shining altars and dreamy chapels? I tell you this is the studio of the arts--their best is here, because inspired from above and consecrated, not to the lewd and charmful of the flesh, but to the picturing, as it may be, of the spirits' beautifullest triumphs in sight of a never-fading crown. This is the house of education by object-lessons, such as only a Mistress of 1,900 years' experience can give the eager humanity, that climbs her lap in every age to suck the sweets of intellectual love.

Here the poor, who hath but given a penny, smiles serenely around upon it all as he claims it rightfully as his own, because he is a son of the family. Here the rich learns to consecrate his wealth to God and mankind—a treasure here and reward hereafter. But, really, we must stick to our theme. I ask your pardon for the seeming neglect of it. We have finished one division of our subject. What good is done the mass of mankind, the working population, by the church?"

Professor: "I beg to remark that your two questions lap over each other. What is all this fine building, painting, sculpture, music, poetry, except for the pleasure and profit of the most numerous of your attendants—the poor?"

O. T. Bee: "But then you mistake the question: it is: What money profit do the poor gain by it?

Thomas: "Why, plainly, I would say, the material part of the work which they do and are paid for. Art is not like selfish riches. She does not disdain to employ the humblest to help her in whatsoever he can. While Dame Wealth sits back and professes to be self-contained and despise the poor, by whose very labor she is rich."

Father: "Well said, Thomas. To bring the matter right down to every man's door—here, take up this advertising pamphlet of a Church Architect. Turn to this city church—St. George's, Chicago. The interior shows a vaulted ceiling, clustered columns with rich caps whence spring pointed arches; transepts, beautiful low altar and self-supporting gallery. How long would it take to build this? How many kinds of workmen would have to be employed? How much money would be expended?

Last question first—over $50,000.

Second, I wish some one would suggest a trade or profession that is *not* represented in the building of this church and its appurtenances."

Thomas: "How would a pile-driver get in his work here?"

Father: "Simply by driving piles if needed by the marshy soil. Try again.

Uncom. Traveler: "Silk factory, or better—now I've got it—journalism."

Thomas: "Out on both counts, our drummer boy. There is more gold and silver, silk and satin, woolen and linen goods used about the altar of a well-furnished Catholic Church than would furnish twenty-five well-to-do families. As to the editor's chair: Why don't you know they actually issue a paper, and no despicable one, from that residence beside the Church?"

Father: "Pass on to Church of Sacred Heart, East Saginaw, Mich. It is a modest but beautiful stone-trimmed Gothic: tower 22 feet square, 170 feet high; the cross on front gable 85 feet from the ground. It has a turret at centre of transept, basement, rich groined ceiling, can contain 1,000 people and costs for building alone $40,000. Calculate again what an ornament such a building must be; how it enhances the price of building lots; spurs on the City Council to brush up the town, speculators to erect expensive stores; enables poor people to get lots of work for months and months—a year or two. And remember, our rule is to *pay* for churches. They can't be consecrated until paid for and have decent support. Turn over and take a more modest example still: St. Mary's, Alexandria, Ky. Now, I'm sure that scarcely one in a dozen will know there is such a town. It is not peculiarly famous, but you may perceive, by this good church—50x100, tower 109 feet, costing $13,000, including lumber, sand and bowlders furnished by the congregation, that, likely enough, there is a thrifty band of German farmers and tradesmen in the ninety families thereabouts."

Uncom. Traveler: "What a boom such people and such a church and school—for I see a fine school too—must be to the little nursling town. How the boomers claim such advantages too when advertising. Why, when I was in Newport News last summer, I went along with the visiting priest to the office of the big Railroad and Steamship Company, and there coolly saw the priest pick out two of the best lots in the map and have it turned over to him for the nominal sum of fifty dollars. 'And this,' said the agent, 'in order that I may tell the other ministers who apply, that I have no free lots to give away—even the Catholic plot was paid for in hard cash!'"

Father: "So it goes. The trades-people and the
railroad magnates know what a large factor the
church is in building up, beautifying and heightening
the value of property and pushing the activity of the
trades and profession, not to wish to see her encouraged—in fact, to make capital out of her, and be
glad of her patronage.

To end — where things seem endless — you just
ought to see the variety of circulars, cards,
advertising papers, etc., etc., which pour in
upon a priest, a school teacher, our Sisters and
Brothers. Examine that drawer; here are catalogues
of books from every corner of the country and from
at least five countries of Europe. A magic lantern
and stereopticon (and there is one in use here too
with English imported slides worth $1.50 apiece),
tailors' measurement book from New York and
Antwerp, Belgium—a 1001 advertising schemes of
regular church dealers—the candle man, the olive-oil
man, the wine-grower, the ecclesiastical haberdasher,
the bell founder, the pew and desk cabinet-maker,
the jeweler, the picture-framer, the music dealer, (by
the scores); the theatre furnisher for exhibitions, the
glass-blower, the brass moulder, the pass-book ped-
dler, the village saddle-bag maker, school-furnisher,
(by the fifties); the cross and bead and religious
trinket vendor. We must not forget the dry goods
merchants, who want to furnish First Communion
suits; and the green grocers, who have a splendid
list of Lenten fare to offer. Finally, the endless and
ceaseless patter of the invitations of cigar manufac-
turers and the snuff-burners. For, if there be a thing
which the priest puts in lieu of almost all amuse-

ments and recreations, from which he is excluded by his cloth, it is his pipe and a good brand of tobacco. So we'll close by smoking the calumet of peace. God bless you all!"

www.ingramcontent.com/pod-product-compliance
Lightning Source LLC
Chambersburg PA
CBHW020750020726
47495CB00008B/2367